Taking Chances

ARIA GLAZKI

ANIKA PRESS

TAKING CHANCES Copyright © 2018
by Aria Glazki

This book is a work of fiction. Names, characters, places, and incidents are either products of the author's imagination or are used fictitiously. Any resemblance to actual persons, living or dead, events, or locales is coincidental. The author makes no claims to, but instead acknowledges the trademarked status and trademark owners of the word marks mentioned in this work of fiction.

Cover design by Paper & Sage
Cover photo by Lorri Lang

ISBN: 978-1-943572-13-7

Taking Chances

One

The even murmur of the crowd didn't change as Liz Anne settled on the stool that marked the makeshift "stage" in a patch of grass. Blowing her nerves out with her breath, she strummed the old guitar, grooves in its neck now molded to her fingertips. Ignoring the blurred faces around her, Liz Anne started into her newest song, letting the steady, calm rhythm settle her heartbeat.

"When the sun sinks down low, and the world goes dark; when I'm broken apart, and I've lost my spark…" Was it her imagination, or had the conversations around her begun to fade? "Desperate I try to believe, somehow you could hear me."

She could feel the eyes on her now. *Just keep playing.* Someone who knew someone had to be among those gathered around this tent, right? She'd tried to time her song early enough that the big names scheduled for the main stage wouldn't yet pull everyone away.

"And whispered pleas fall from my lips…"

The final notes allowed her a few seconds to steel herself before lifting the guitar from her lap, pasting on a confident smile, and standing to give up the stool to any other interested singers. A smattering of applause acknowledged her performance.

Stepping out of the cleared area, Liz Anne focused only on keeping her mind blank, blocking any intruding hopes that maybe, this time…

A duo had already replaced her, and Liz Anne hovered at the outside edges of the small crowd, pretending to listen like they probably had while waiting their turn. Her free hand snaked through the casual waves of her hair that she'd painstakingly styled this morning. *Whatever it takes.*

Bobby let out a sliding whistle, his eyes following a swaying set of hips in barely there short shorts that showed off lean, long legs. "I sure don't get tired of this."

"Eyes in your head," Steve said, all too predictably.

But in this sea of flannel, denim, and smiles, Bobby didn't even mind. And he definitely didn't plan on listening. "We got some time. Why not enjoy the local talent," he goaded with a grin.

"At least pretend you care about the music."

Scraps of melodies floated around them as they meandered around the festival booths. Bobby did care, about their music—playing with Steve and Kane. Scouring the pop-up hopefuls' showcases wasn't his thing. Kane had been thinking about adding an opener to their gigs, but finding someone was up to Mitch. All Bobby was good for was playing.

But the women didn't mind, and the beer was good. What else did a guy need?

A mix of anxiety and anticipation thrummed through Liz Anne, tapping itself out on her well-worn guitar case. Her gaze swept the clusters of people, her lips forcing a pleasant smile any time she made eye contact. An older man with graying hair and a dark suit jacket looked her down and up before his eyes narrowed on her face. Liz Anne's cheeks tightened with her smile. You never knew who was somebody in this town, even if this festival wasn't actually *in* Nashville.

The man smiled in return and headed toward her. She shifted her weight into one hip and flattened a palm on the top of the case standing beside her.

"Not bad," the man said, planting himself in front of her.

Was he talking about her music or…? "Thanks," she said brightly.

"Got any more?"

"More?" she echoed.

"Songs," he clarified, hitching a thumb into one of his jean pockets.

Liz Anne's lips popped open. *No way.* "Yes, of—of course."

Silence fell between them. Was he a manager? A talent scout? He might expect her to know, but not living in Nashville put her at a serious disadvantage when it came to knowing the players. Then again, he might be no one, trying to take advantage of the countless girls here like her, hoping for someone to give them a shot. But Liz Anne had too much at stake to be an easy mark.

"C'mon." He tilted his head away from the people focused on the impromptu "stage" she'd recently occupied.

"Where's that, mister…?" Liz Anne asked, not moving.

"Dennings. Mitch." The corner of his lips tugged up into a smirk. "I'd like to hear another song or two." Doubt must have shown on her face because he added, "You ever hear of Kane Hartridge?"

"Sure." She nodded to back up the lie. Much as she loved her music, she didn't exactly have the spare time to keep up with every new singer or band trying to make their way. She stuck with her favorites, or whoever caught her ear on the radio.

"Well, he's looking for an opener," Mitch Dennings said. "Think you got what it takes?"

Shoot. Slimy shoot on an extra-stale cracker. Mitch Dennings stood talking something over in hushed tones with another man, both of them sending glances Liz Anne's way that she pretended not to notice. There was plenty to fake-focus on— people strolling by and colorful booths and a breeze that played with anything that moved. But their conversation didn't look like good news for her. She shouldn't have let the stranger get her hopes up, even if it did seem like he might really be a manager.

The men stopped talking and turned toward her, and Liz Anne shot them both her friendliest smile. One good thing about being a waitress: you learned to smile no matter what mess of emotions was churning in your gut.

"Kane Hartridge," Mr. Dennings said when they reached her, "this here's Liz Anne…" His eyes widened a fraction as he trailed off.

"Layton. It's a–an honor to meet you, Mr. Hartridge."

The singer's—*Lord, please let him really be a singer*—eyes crinkled at the corners. Was he laughing at her? She forced her smile to tick up another notch.

"You a fan?" he asked. Younger than the manager, he still had a good decade on her.

Liz Anne's answer came out as half–affirmation, half-hum. "You bet," she added.

Hartridge's eyes narrowed, losing their edge of humor. Whatever he'd wanted her to say, that hadn't been it.

She sighed, dropping the false smile. Sweat slickened her grip on her guitar case. "No, I'm sorry, I'm actually not. Not that I don't like your music," she added quickly. "I don't rightly know. I'm not sure I've ever heard any of it, to be honest. But I'm sure it's great—you're…great." Her head shook as her mind caught up to her rambling. "I'm awfully sorry to waste your time." She managed another tight smile then lifted the case, focusing on the trampled grass below her boots.

"Hold on, now," the singer said before she'd managed to do more than turn around. So much for a pain-free getaway.

She hitched her shoulders back and twisted around to face them again.

"You write your own songs?" he asked.

"I do." Any second of spare time she could scrounge up was devoted to scribbling down lyrics or working out melodies.

"All right." Hartridge scanned behind her for something, and Liz Anne held her breath, not moving, like a scared little bunny. Her heart was pounding something awful, too. With a nod, he gestured behind her, a bit to the left.

Inhaling, she spotted a couple fold-up chairs behind a booth with scarves and hats, out of the way of the main path. A pinch of tension left her stance as she picked her way over, followed by the men. Good thing she'd decided on jeans instead of her cutoff shorts, or her legs would've burned up on a metal chair left out in the sun.

After watching her take out the guitar and start to tune—near impossible under their scrutiny—the men took a few steps away and resumed their hushed conversation. It took them a few moments to notice when she'd finally gotten the instrument ready. Hartridge took half a step back toward her, his attention politely if distantly trained on her.

Liz Anne strummed a couple chords, willing her heart to stop beating so hard it'd throw off her rhythm, then flexed her fingers for good measure. Her breath blew out steadily over the opening chords. She made a last-minute decision to ditch the song's first few lines, then started, "I walk the line of wrong or right, and I know where I stand. Holding true to my values, you may not understand. But I don't care."

Humming the next measure, she risked a glance at the men currently deciding her future. Or maybe having a laugh. The manager was looking over her shoulder, back toward the booths. Hartridge was frowning.

"Under the Good Lord's watchful eye, don't dare—" Her fingers hit a wrong note, and now Hartridge was shaking his head.

Liz Anne palmed the vibrating strings and stopped singing.

The singer watched her a moment before speaking. "It's just not ready." A thread of pity underscored the words.

Liz Anne nodded quickly. "Okay." Her lips defaulted to that professional smile. "Thank you for your time."

Bobby elbowed Steve, then jerked his chin in Kane and Mitch's direction. Or more accurately, in the direction of the girl sitting in front of them holding a guitar. He could get behind another singer joining them if they looked like her.

"Wouldn't get your hopes up," Steve said.

Bobby scowled. "Why not?"

"'Cause Kane makes his decisions with a different part of his anatomy than you do."

"Maybe she's good." Though now that they'd gotten closer, she looked more terrified than talented. Real pretty, though, with her long blonde hair—and even longer legs.

"Didn't sound like the song you played earlier," Mitch was saying when they got in earshot.

Kane nodded to them, but the girl bristled, her gaze bouncing between the four of them before landing on Kane.

"Uhm, yeah," she said. "If you don't mind, I could try that other one?"

"Sure." But it didn't sound like Kane expected much.

Steve shot Bobby a "what'd I tell you?" look. How bad had whatever she'd already played been? Oh well. Maybe she'd need some comforting after hearing Kane's decision. It wasn't like Bobby had anywhere he had to be for the next couple of hours.

The girl's gaze swept the four of them again, and Bobby shot her a smile for good measure. She immediately focused all her attention on her guitar, blowing her breath out between pursed lips as her fingers twitched lightly above the strings.

She strummed a chord twice, switched to another, then switched back before starting to sing a soft ballad. "When the sun sinks down low, and the world goes dark…"

Bobby looked to the other men, but they were watching the girl. Not that he blamed them, but what was he missing here? She sounded pretty good. Could use some work on the guitar, maybe, make the line more interesting than the basic chords, but still. It didn't make sense, Kane looking so uninterested.

"Desperate I try to believe…somehow you could hear me. Quiet pleas fall from my lips, fly from my lips to heaven."

She was definitely on to something there, about her lips and heaven. Bobby shifted his weight onto his right leg. As she moved into the second verse, Kane held up a hand. She stopped mid-word, her lips still parted.

"All right. How about we find a time, better place, so we can listen properly," Kane said.

Those lips moved into a tiny smile before she asked, "Really?"

"Boys," Mitch said, half-waving at Steve and Bobby, "this here's Liz Anne. Steve's our drummer,"—Steve ducked his chin toward her—"and Bobby's on bass guitar."

"Pleasure," Bobby said.

Liz Anne smiled more broadly, nodding back toward them.

"Talk it over with Mitch, find a time." Kane pulled his phone out, glancing at it briefly. "It was good meeting you. Excuse me." He didn't stick around for Liz Anne's response, which probably meant it was Sabella calling. Nothing short of a show could make Kane miss his wife's calls, not that she called when they were on stage anyway.

Liz Anne and Mitch started talking schedules, and Bobby turned to Steve. "Told ya."

"What're you so excited about?" the drummer asked.

"Did you see her?"

Steve shook his head with his "I'm so much smarter than you" smirk. "Two ways this can go. He says no, and she heads on home with her hopes and dreams crushed, with no mind for anything else. Or, by some miracle he says yes. And then she's off limits."

"Well, shoot." Bobby started to frown, but Steve wasn't seeing option number three: all that time before she played for Kane again. "Ain't no harm in being friendly in the meanwhile, is there?"

Two

Once they'd agreed on a time for Liz Anne's second semi-audition, the men went off to work, or enjoy the festival, or more than likely to look for someone better to play for them. Only the bass guitarist stuck around as she snapped the latch closed on her guitar case.

"Looks like we both have a bit of free time," he said with a confident smile when Liz Anne straightened.

Curly hair and a lanky build, infinitely comfortable in his own skin, and a smile filled with carefree mischief. Exactly the kind of guy who could get a girl in trouble. "Only kind of playing I'm interested in is music, all right?"

He splayed his hands out in front of him. "All right. Maybe I could help you out, then. For when you play for Kane again."

"How's that?"

His smile ticked up a notch, and his head tilted toward the bustle of the fair. "You hungry?"

Not in the least, with all the nerves twisting her gut up into a tangled mess. What she really needed to do was find somewhere to listen to Kane Hartridge's music. Maybe it'd help her figure out what song to play for him, if she had something that matched his sound. But she couldn't exactly afford to alienate one of his band members, either. Any little thing could tip the scales against her. "Sure. Why not?"

"You could sound a little more excited at my generous offer," the guitarist said as they headed toward the picnic area and its surrounding food booths.

"You really want to help me? Tell me about Kane's music."

"What about it?"

She shrugged, then passed her free hand through her hair to resettle it back away from her face. "Anything."

He stopped mid-step, swinging around to look at her, confusion just under the surface of his expression. "You ain't never heard of Kane?"

Oh, sugar honey iced tea. How big a deal was he? "Let's just say I don't make it out all that much."

"Now I see. You're using me for a crash course, get the inside scoop." A cheeky smirk accompanied the accusation.

Liz Anne chuckled, shaking her head as they resumed walking. "Nothing a quick Google search wouldn't be able to tell me."

"Well, shoot. Reckon I can do more for you than that."

There was something intense about Liz Anne. Focused, like every move she made was the most important thing in the world. Even now, as she listened to some songs Bobby'd pulled up, her hand resting protectively on her guitar case, her eyes were focused on something abstract in the distance, lips pinched like she was analyzing every second of the music.

Usually Bobby had no problem getting a girl to relax. But this one was barely paying attention to him. Or to the great, sunny day around them. "You know what," he said, standing up from the picnic table, "I'm gonna get us a couple beers."

She pulled one of the buds out of her ear, but barely glanced at him to say, "No, thanks."

"I don't mind."

She fixed him with a no-nonsense look, pulling the other ear bud out. "I don't drink."

"You're kidding." *Unless…* "You are over twenty-one, right?"

She rolled her eyes rather than answer. "There's more to life than alcohol."

"Yeah." He braced his hands on the table, leaning toward her with his foolproof smile. "There's also music. And fine women like you."

She didn't move, but a new tension filled her posture, a wariness sharpening her gaze.

Bobby straightened, hitching his weight into one hip and tucking his thumbs in his pockets. "You all right, there?"

She blinked quickly, that odd stillness fading away, like she'd just started breathing again. "Right as rain. If you want that beer, don't let me stop you." She held his phone back out to him.

"If you say so." He could tell when he wasn't wanted. Plenty other fish, and all that. Plus Steve might've had a point about unnecessary complications. "See ya 'round, then."

"Oh I'm free, free without you." Liz Anne let her last chord sound for a couple of seconds, then pressed her palm to the guitar, silencing it. She waited another beat before raising her head to look at Kane Hartridge and his manager. His bandmates had also wandered into the "backstage" area as she played, but they weren't the ones who mattered, not now anyway. Dennings looked like he'd lost interest in whatever made him approach her. Kane was frowning. Not outright, but there was that hint of the edges of his lips being pulled down. The hope that had been trickling through all her attempts to block it out finally stopped fighting reality. The rejection was even worse now that she knew his music was good—really good.

Kane sighed and took a step toward her. Much as she wanted to cower behind her guitar, Liz Anne lifted it away, resting it on the ground as she stood.

"Listen," he said, "you have a good look, a fine voice. Your songs aren't bad, they'll get there. But you're just not ready." He paused, pity deepening that frown. "It's nothing personal, all right?"

"To you." The words slipped out on accident, but there was nothing for it now. Liz Anne pulled her shoulders back and notched her chin up. It was still true.

"What's that?" he asked.

She could almost feel the other men staring at her, shocked. Expecting her to take it back. "It's nothing personal to you. This is incredibly personal to me."

Kane's severe expression didn't change as he took in her stance and stalled on her face, staring her down. But if he thought that'd be enough to make her back down, he was sorely mistaken. She had years of practice handling worse. And the worst thing he could say to her was another "no."

"Kane," the manager said from behind him.

The singer's jaw shifted, breaking the tension built between them, letting Liz Anne inhale. She bit down, clamping her jaw shut to stop herself from blowing the breath out and showing all of them just how nervous she was.

"All right," Kane said, taking a minute step back. He half-turned to glance at his manager before adding, "One show. Three songs. Next one's out in Evansville. Mitch'll give you details. Prove me wrong."

She'd barely nodded before he turned his attention to his bandmates. "Time?" he asked them.

She didn't hear their answer because Dennings had stepped closer, saying, "All right, then. Evansville's next Friday, you can be there?"

She couldn't not be there. But was there something planned she was forgetting? She'd just have to make it work. "Uh—yeah. Yes," she told the manager, a bit too late.

"You sure, now?"

Kane had already said no twice, but even one real show opening for him was better than the nothing she'd done 'til then. The bass guitarist paused in his tuning, shooting her a smile behind the manager's back, but Liz Anne focused on the older man who'd helped make this happen. "Absolutely."

"Hi, Momma," Liz Anne said, softly shutting the front door.

Her momma put down the pants she was mending and slipped off her glasses.

Liz Anne tucked her guitar behind the old sofa and asked, "He asleep?" At her momma's nod, she added, "Thank you for letting me go today."

"Didn't expect you to be gone all day."

"I know. Me either." Liz Anne gave her momma a beat, in case she wanted to ask about the festival. When the silence kept on, Liz Anne made her way over to the kitchen to pour herself some home-made sweet tea. "You want some, Momma?"

"No."

Liz Anne took a deep breath before joining her momma at the table. How was it Momma's silence could still make her feel like a high schooler?

"You gonna tell me how it went?"

She sipped the tea to wet her suddenly parched mouth. It was good news, but it wasn't going to be easy on them. "It went good. There's this singer, he wants me to open for him next week." That was stretching the truth a bit, but her momma didn't need to know she'd basically begged him for another chance. "On Friday."

Momma nodded, picking up the mending again.

"You—you don't need the car or nothing?"

"This a real singer?" she asked, showing no emotion at the news. Not that Liz Anne could blame her. Any time she spent away from home meant everything falling on her momma's shoulders, like today.

"Yeah. He is. Want me to boot up the computer? Play you something? He's really good." He actually was, with real fans and everything. The manager had said something about them heading on tour, too. It was why they wanted an opener. But Liz Anne wasn't holding her breath for anything more than the one night. She just had to make sure she didn't embarrass herself up on stage.

"No. It's late." Momma snipped the thread, folded up the pants, and put away her sewing supplies. "I'm fixing to head to bed. Don't forget to have some supper."

"Okay." Really, she was too tired to eat, but there was no use making it into an argument.

As Momma headed toward the bedrooms, she paused, hand landing on Liz Anne's shoulder. She squeezed gently. "We'll work out Friday."

Liz Anne placed her hand over the worn, familiar one. Her momma might not always approve, but she always came through. "Thanks, Momma."

Alone in the silent, dimly lit living room, Liz Anne lifted her arms overhead and stretched for a beat, before letting them drop with a sharp exhale. She'd have to get someone to cover her shift Friday, and find some extra time to practice over the coming days. Meanwhile, it was back to real life. And that meant getting herself to bed for a couple hours' rest before her dawn wakeup call.

With a sigh, she shoved back from the table and circled the living room to turn out the lights. A faint glow shone down the hallway leading to the bedrooms. Liz Anne pushed open her door, careful not to make a sound. Parker was lying still, his blanket tangled around one foot. The nightlight he still needed was bright enough that she didn't switch on the ceiling lamp. The sight of his curly hair and peaceful expression made her smile despite her own exhaustion.

She bent over his bed, tugging the blanket back up around his shoulders, then lowered to the floor, her palm resting on his chest, feeling the steady rise and fall of his breathing. All the reasons in the world to give up, but he was the only one she needed not to. She had to show him that pursuing your dreams mattered, no matter the dirty whispers and judging looks of everyone in town. Making something more of herself than a waitress down at Walt's Diner, that was the only way she could take her son away from Fairview's small-town minds, who cared more for spreading rumors and feeling superior than just about anything else, even if that meant making life hard for a little kid who was nothing but innocent. Liz Anne would do anything to build a better life for Parker. Maybe, if she made it big enough, someday she could buy them all a place in Nash- ville. For him and her momma.

Three

"Well I'll be. Hey, Steve!" Bobby called across the small parking lot. He grinned when the drummer made eye contact. "Looks like you owe me a twenty."

They'd bet on whether Liz Anne would actually show up. Steve thought she'd chicken out, too embarrassed, but Bobby'd seen the steel in her spine. And he'd been right.

There she was, eyes bouncing between them as Steve unpacked his drums from the truck. Mitch was inside, talking something over with the booker or the sound tech, and Kane had gone off as soon as his wife called, but who could blame him. Sabella was about the best thing that ever happened to him, but she still spent a fair bit of time out on the West Coast.

Steve started moving toward the door Bobby had propped open, but Liz Anne stalled in the middle of the lot.

She looked great, in her skintight jeans and a pale tank top with a few buttons down the center of her chest. All buttoned, of course. Her hair was down again, flowing over her shoulders and almost down to her waist.

"You all right there?" Bobby called to her.

She hesitated a moment, but then offered him a sort of plastic smile. "Just wondering where y'all want me."

Well now, if that wasn't an invitation…

"Go on inside," Steve said before Bobby could do something stupid. But they had a show to put on.

Liz Anne's shoulders pulled back, her posture damn near perfect as she took measured steps toward the bar's side entrance.

"Good to see you again," Bobby said politely as he could when she passed him.

She paused, her light-blue eyes looking up at him. "Glad to be here," she said, but those eyes were drowning in fear.

Those same nerves still visibly jangled through Liz Anne hours later as Mitch introduced their "special guest." Bobby bent toward her ear. "Deep breath. They won't bite."

She tore her eyes off the stage to look up at him. The tension didn't disappear at his teasing, but at least she inhaled. Halfway there.

Her lips pursed as she blew the breath out, making her way toward the mic Mitch had used. She settled on the stool, strumming her guitar once before silencing it.

"Hi, y'all. I ain't here to talk your ear off, so I just want to say a quick thank you to Kane, and to all y'all for having me here." She stared out at the smattering of people. Mitch now stood with Kane by the bar, checking out her set. Bobby stayed off to the side with Steve.

"This is a uh, a new song." She cleared her throat then offered the room a playful smile. "But I think a few of the ladies here tonight might be able to relate." Folks didn't react much, but still she struck the first chord and started singing. "Met you in a bar, they said we won't go far, I should have listened. No it didn't take long—a new girl came along, and you went missing."

It wasn't a bad call, starting with a pretty straight-up song of a woman wronged, the one she'd played for Kane, but the guitar line was still beyond basic. Rough. So easily fleshed out, the expanded line played in Bobby's head as Liz Anne sang.

"She has something," he said to Steve.

"Long legs and blonde hair aren't going to cut it for Kane," the drummer answered.

Bobby frowned. Did he not hear it? Sure, Liz Anne was hot, but there was something else, too.

"Hand me another drink," she said, breaking the melody, and a couple people laughed before she dove back into the chorus. She faded the song out with echoes of the lyrics, a bit too serious for the rest of the song, but it could be spruced up with that stronger guitar part. Steve might not see it, but if Bobby did, it was a pretty sure bet Kane would, too.

Liz Anne hit the final beat of her third song, following it up with a slow, deep breath. She'd done it. The people at the tables weren't exactly cheering their hearts out, but they'd clapped a bit. And she'd gotten through all three songs.

"Thank you," she said into the mic, sneaking a look to her left to make sure Kane and the others were ready. Shooting the room a practiced smile, she added, "And now, for the reason all y'all are here, and me too, if we're honest, please welcome the fantastic Kane Hartridge."

The applause amped up. She slipped off the stool, crossing behind Kane as he took his place center stage.

"Pretty good," Bobby said to her as they passed each other.

It shouldn't have mattered, but the approval bubbled warmly in her chest. Her first real gig, and it hadn't been a huge mess. How many folks had even gotten that far?

Behind her, Kane and the others launched into an upbeat song, not one of the ones she'd listened to already. Liz Anne focused on putting away her guitar as the nerves she'd pushed aside buzzed through her.

"Hope you're sticking around," Dennings said, and she nearly jumped.

"Oh, of—of course." She'd figured rushing out right after would look rude. And anyway, it would be nice to hang out a bit, watch Kane play. "Did he have a chance to say anything?" she asked the manager, angling toward the stage respectfully.

Dennings looked her up and down quickly, like a judge more than a man, then focused on the band. "Not yet."

She nodded, mind racing, and fixed another smile on her face. She'd known going in that this would probably be the only time she'd open for Kane. And she wouldn't let that ruin her chance to enjoy a night of good country singing.

The people who'd sort of paid attention to her songs had started singing along with Kane, some even shifting tables around to stand closer. He followed up the first song with a mid-tempo one about some good old summer fun, and Liz Anne let herself slip away into the music.

Bobby handed Kane a fresh beer, interrupting him and Liz Anne chatting in the corner. The beer could've waited, but Bobby wanted an excuse to hear Kane's decision. After tonight, he had to see Liz Anne would be a fine choice of opener, with a little help, maybe.

Kane tipped the bottle in Bobby's direction, then took a long sip. Bobby offered Liz Anne one of the other bottles he held, but she waved it away with a tense smile.

"Like I was saying," Kane said, shooting Bobby a look he cheerfully ignored, "you do have potential. With some more guitar work, a couple more gigs under your belt, maybe next year you can join us."

"Okay." Liz Anne's nod kept on like a bobble-head toy, crestfallen behind her polite smile. "Thanks so much for the shot."

"You stay in touch, all right?" Kane said.

"Well, hang on a second," Bobby heard himself interrupting. Both of the singers turned to look at him. Kane's eyes narrowed, and Liz Anne's just jumped between the men. "I can help her out with the guitar parts, and there's still time before we go out, for her to sing some. The Commodore, some other places."

"Two weeks, Bobby. It's not enough time." Kane looked back to Liz Anne. "I'm sorry."

She parted her lips to give him what would no doubt be another bland mix of disappointed thank-yous.

"It's plenty of time." Bobby grinned in response to Kane's frown. "I can teach anybody."

Kane shook his head lightly, tipping the beer to his lips again. "Listen," he said, mostly to Liz Anne, "I can't make any promises. We need to find someone who's ready to go on right away. But Bobby here's an okay guitar player, so if you're serious about this, I'd take him up on that offer."

Liz Anne nodded nervously, the muscles in her neck straining a bit as she swallowed.

"And I'll talk to Amber Lynn and some folks, see about getting you some open mic spots sooner than later. All right?"

"Thank you," Liz Anne rushed to say.

Kane dipped his chin, then turned to tell Bobby, "Five minutes," and walked off to help Steve chat up the fans in the time left before their second set.

"Why're you doing this?" Liz Anne asked Bobby the moment Kane was out of earshot.

"What, no 'thank you' for me?"

"I don't need your help." She was being rude, but she still grit her jaw and notched up her chin.

"Well that clearly ain't true. Now I don't know if you noticed, but I'm actually pretty good at this whole playing thing. So I help you spruce up your songs a bit." He shrugged. "No big deal."

"In exchange for what?"

His lips curved into a lazy, victorious smirk. "I'll take that 'thank you,' for starters."

Liz Anne swallowed. No question he wanted something more. He wasn't bad-looking or anything. But how far was she willing to go to make it?

Not that far.

Bobby's smirk slipped into a scowl, and he took a half step back, squinting at her. "Just wanted to help out. You'd think no one ain't ever done anything nice for you before."

"Not without a price." Her brain caught up a second too late, and she pressed her lips together.

He paused a minute, sizing her up, but then that cheeky smile found his face again. "Good thing you met me then, ain't it?" He slipped his phone out. "Now how 'bout you give me your number before I have to get back out there."

"Why don't you give me yours?" she asked, biting back a returning smile. Maybe she had her guard up just a bit too high.

He leaned in like he was about to share a secret with her, his face intimately close. "We both know I won't be the one to chicken out." With a quick lift of his eyebrows, he left the phone in her hands and went to grab his guitar.

She stared at the device. Truth be had, she couldn't remember all that much about his playing, too amped up by the whole night. But if he was offering to help, if this could help her get better and there really was nothing else going on, didn't she have to take him up on it? She'd try just about anything to get Parker the life he deserved. If it didn't feel right the first time, she'd back out and that would be that.

$\mathcal{F}our$

Saturday afternoon, Liz Anne's phone buzzed once against her thigh as she set two loaded plates on the diner's laminated table. They weren't supposed to keep their phones on at work, but she wasn't taking any chances with Parker, even when he was safe with her momma.

Liz Anne wished a quick, "Enjoy your meal," to the man sitting alone by the window, then made her way to the back so she could check the message.

```
Free tonight?
```

Bobby. She'd called herself after giving him the number, so she wouldn't be surprised. Should she pretend she hadn't? Ask who it was?

Don't be stupid. She had more important things to worry about than playing coy. Her shift wouldn't be done until eight. Most Saturdays, she barely made it home to tuck Parker in for the night. So if Momma didn't have any plans, which—thanks to Liz Anne, mostly—she usually didn't, Liz Anne could make it into Nashville a little after nine.

With a deep breath, she reread the words and hit SEND.

"Hey," Addie said, almost bumping into Liz Anne in her rush, "you got a table waiting."

"Thanks," she threw over her shoulder before dropping the phone into her apron pocket and getting back to work.

"You're late," Bobby teased as Liz Anne bent over to grab her guitar from her passenger seat. Her thin sweater hung loose around her torso, but the worn jeans were hugging her curves.

"Sorry," she said immediately, before catching sight of his expression. She shook her head, rolling her eyes at him. "Thanks for doing this so late."

Nine thirty on a Saturday was late? Kane and them had only finished up around two this morning, and that was a quiet night. "Not a problem." Bobby stepped back inside, holding the door open as she came up the steps to his porch. "Come on in."

It looked like she would bolt. But then her shoulders straightened, and she stepped inside like she was about to face a firing squad. Bobby bit back his laugh. He had his work cut out, getting her to relax some, that was for sure. He shut the door and gestured to the couch a few steps away.

"Get you anything?" he asked when she sat down gingerly, drawing the guitar case to her like a shield.

"No, thank you." That polite plastic smile was back.

"Okay, then." Bobby walked over to his worn leather armchair and picked up the waiting guitar. He leaned forward and grabbed the beer he'd left on the low table. "Shall we?"

The question snapped her into motion, and soon her instrument rested on her lap.

"All right," Bobby said, "let's see what you got. Try and follow along with me." He played a basic two-finger exercise leading up the strings and down a higher pitch, then looked to his anxious student.

She took a deep breath, then started painstakingly picking through the same pattern.

"Hold on," he interrupted. "You're more a strummer, I'm guessing."

She held his gaze with a blank look, her lips pressing together.

"How 'bout you play me one of your songs, for a jumping off point." He hadn't exactly been paying attention to her technique last night. "What's that quiet one you played? Something about heaven."

She nodded then stared down at her guitar a few moments before starting to strum a D chord, up and down. She switched to G, keeping that steady pace. But most of the motion came from her wrist, making the chord uneven.

Bobby set aside his guitar and moved over to the couch. She startled, staring at him over her shoulder instead of starting to sing. The guitar fell silent. "I don't bite," he said.

"Maybe I do," she told him, those blue eyes not backing down. With her hair pulled back like tonight, there was nothing to distract from her eyes, her mouth, the line of her neck.

Bobby swallowed and focused on her right hand. "Your strumming motion's a bit off." He took her wrist lightly and sent her forearm through the right motion, an even strum from the elbow. "See? No swiveling your wrist." He let go. "Try it."

She started again like before, then stopped herself and focused on the motion, bringing out a better sound. She paused to switch chords.

"Who taught you to play?" he asked.

She stopped entirely, resting her fingering hand on her lap. "No one, really. An old boyfriend showed me some chords, once. But by the time I got a guitar, I'd forgotten them. So I looked some up, started messing around on my own." She shrugged. "Doesn't mean I can't do this."

"Three chords and the truth," Bobby said quietly. It was a nice idea, and there was something to it, but… "But that ain't really going to cut it."

She frowned. "If you don't want to help, I get it—"

"Slow down. Just—" He shifted back to the chair and picked up his own guitar again. "Look, play your song again. Don't worry about the strumming, just try and listen to what I play."

He waited for her to get through a few lines, getting a fresh feel for the song, before starting to pick out little embellishments to her chords. Her frown grew deeper, wrinkling between her eyebrows. Bobby simplified the line he was playing to a different rhythm of the same chords she was using.

She stopped playing after the second verse, her lips parted as she watched him.

He stopped too at her slightly stunned look. "Maybe I've got something to teach you after all, huh?"

Her lips twitched with a half-exhaled chuckle. "I'm sorry if I've seemed…ungrateful. I really do appreciate you taking the time to help, when you don't have to."

"Always up for a challenge," he joked, but her head dropped. He leaned forward to brush her knee. "I was kidding."

She nodded, but not like she believed him. "Right."

Something softer than usual flashed in her eyes, but a second later she pulled those shoulders ramrod straight, any trace of vulnerability gone.

"Well, listen," Bobby said, leaning back, "I can give you some finger exercises and all that if you want. But I think the easiest way to help your songs is to play with your rhythm a bit. Get it a little less even, so it feels more like a song than a march."

"Okay," she agreed more easily, resettling her guitar on her lap.

At least he'd convinced her he knew what he was doing. "All right, let's do it."

<h1 style="text-align:center">Five</h1>

The bed jostling snapped Liz Anne out of sleep the next morning. A blurred face swam before her as her eyes struggled to focus.

"Whatcha doin'?" she asked, pulling Parker down to the bed. She held him close for a moment before moving back to tickle him. He squealed, the light laughter smoothing away any lingering stresses from the week. Sunday mornings were their time, no matter what else was going on.

"Sto-op," he giggled after a minute. They both flopped on their backs, staring at the ceiling.

Liz Anne took a deep breath, giving herself one more moment before diving into the day. "Okay, baby." She pushed herself up, then rolled her son out of bed and followed him to the bathroom.

"What're we doing today?" he asked around his toothbrush.

"We are brushing our teeth," she said to get the bristles moving again. She squeezed paste onto her own toothbrush before adding, "And then, how 'bout some pancakes?"

"Yeah!" He pulled the bright-red plastic out of his mouth.

"Ah—teeth first," she directed, swallowing a smile.

Pretty soon they stood by the stove, still in their PJs but with a big bowl of batter all ready to go.

Liz Anne flicked some water onto the skillet, and a hiss filled the air. She turned to her son, who was not-so-secretly licking batter off his fingers. "You ready?" she asked, positioning him in front of the stove. She helped him ladle a big plop of batter onto the skillet. His fingers dug into the waiting smaller bowl, scooping up a handful of chocolate chips that he threw into the pancake-to-be. He reached for more chips, and she dropped a hand onto his shoulder. "I think that's enough chocolate for this one, don't you?"

His face slipped into a tiny pout, for just a second, before he asked, "Can I flip it?"

"Not yet, you see any bubbles?"

"There's one!" His finger reached toward the blip of air.

"Parker!" Liz Anne instantly pulled him back, dropping the spatula she'd had waiting. It clattered to the floor as she stilled her breath. "You know you can't touch things on the stove."

His expression fell into a heartbreaking mix of hurt and fear. "I'm sorry."

She crouched next to him, running her palms up and down his arms. "You could've been hurt. You okay?"

He nodded, his lips pressed shut.

"How's about I flip this one myself, and you go on and get us some orange juice." She grabbed the spatula off the floor and stood, steering him gently toward the fridge. As her heart settled, she plucked a clean spatula from the old ceramic pitcher—colored with sharpies by Liz Anne in grade school, though Momma refused to throw it out—and flipped the burning pancake.

Parker slid the carton of juice onto the counter beside her, staying a few steps away. She wrapped an arm around him as she brought down some glasses. "It's okay, baby. We just need to be careful near the stove, okay?" She handed him a filled glass, then slid the pancake onto the waiting plate. "'Cause if we get hurt, we have to spend the whole day at the doctor's, instead of having fun. And I dunno 'bout you," she added, ladling out more batter and holding the chocolate chips out for him, "but I'd rather have pancakes than see a doctor. What d'you think?"

"Yeah." He reached for the bowl, standing on tiptoes to toss the chips at the waiting batter from a ways away. "Pancakes for sure."

Parker's eyes stayed trained on the skillet while her phone buzzed on the counter. Liz Anne poured herself some orange juice as she flipped it over.

You practicing?

A second message popped up a moment later.

Might be a pop quiz at our next lesson 😉

She flipped the phone back over, sliding it away on the counter before getting back to the pancakes. But a small smile tugged at her lips.

"That's getting better," Bobby told Liz Anne Monday night as she ran through the basic finger exercises he'd shown her. He set the water she'd accepted down next to his beer, and pulled his guitar into his lap.

She looked up at him with a murmured, "Thank you." Smudges of darkness underscored her eyes, but Bobby wasn't into prying.

"You wanna jump right in?" he asked.

"It's why we're here." She pulled the guitar closer, curving her torso over it to see the frets. She placed her fingers to start playing the song they'd been working on, and ran the other hand over the strings to test out the chord.

"You gotta stop doing that."

She startled, turning to him. "Uhm, what?"

"You all right today?"

She immediately glued a smile on her face. "Yeah, yep. Right as rain, why?"

"Seem a little worn out." He reached for a slice of the chocolate-frosted cake squares she'd brought over. "You should take a break."

"We just started," she pointed out with widened eyes, like he was a bit dumb.

He took a big bite, swigging some beer to go with it. "This is pretty good," he said with a teasing smile.

But she was back in no-nonsense mode. "Listen, I really appreciate you helping me, teaching me. But I was wondering... D'you think you could take a look at some of my other songs? 'From My Lips' can't be the only one you could"—she tried to flash him a flattering smile, but it only made her look more worn out—"save."

"Yeah, listen." He cleared his throat, setting the rest of his piece of cake down on a waiting paper towel. "That one, it's a little easier. Slow, simple. Easy changes for a big difference. Can't fix all of them by Thursday."

Confusion flashed on her face, and she let the guitar tilt away from her body. "What's on Thursday?"

"Kane got you a spot, at an open mic night." Bobby grinned. "Over at the Commodore Grill."

Her face paled as her mouth popped open. "Thursday?" she repeated, panicked. "I...I can't." She shook her head lightly, as if to make her point.

He'd felt that way the first few times he'd performed, too. But the rush of a responding crowd was well worth the price of nerves. "You'll be fine," he assured. "It's just one open mic night." She was really panicking, over nothing. "Look, I can't tomorrow, but we can get together Wednesday, maybe a couple hours on Thursday, and go through your songs, brush them up."

He dropped a hand on her shoulder, but she stiffened, so he lifted it to the back of the couch. "Getting a spot so quickly doesn't happen every day. This is good news, and it'll be good for you."

She brushed his words off with another headshake, closing her eyes briefly. "I can't meet you any earlier than this."

He snorted, leaning back into the couch. "What do you mean?"

"I'm sure you have better things to do." She'd slipped back into her polite, emotionless shell. "I shouldn't be wasting your time."

"I offered."

"And I have a day job," she snapped. "Responsibilities…"

"More important than your music?" Bobby asked. "'Cause then you're in the wrong business."

She swallowed, her eyes dropping away to the floor. Her hand came to her forehead, pausing for a moment, but then she brushed it through her hair, tucking a loose lock behind her ear as if that was all she meant to do.

"It's 'cause you're a vampire, isn't it?" Bobby said.

She blinked a few times, looking at him again. "What?"

"You ain't available during the day. You don't drink, and so far as I know, don't eat. Hell, you didn't even answer me Sunday 'til pretty late, and I know it ain't 'cause you were at church until sundown." He let his lips find the smirk girls loved. "Only thing that makes sense."

Bewildered amusement seemed to have replaced her panic. "We met during the day," she pointed out, as if he'd really forgotten.

"Oh yeah. There was that."

She chucked breathlessly, looking at him like one of them was crazy and she couldn't decide who.

"Listen, you buy me a beer Thursday night, and I'll play with you. If you want."

"Oh, I…" The humor from a moment ago seeped away. "I can't pay you nothing."

"You mean I ain't getting paid for all this? Well, shoot. Better have me some more of this cake, then." He picked up another square and held it out for her.

She shot him a small but real smile, setting the guitar aside as she took the cake. "Thank you."

Six

*L*iz Anne blew a long breath out between puffed lips, shaking the nerves from her hands before curling her fingers into fists. Adrenaline coursed through her, jittering out her limbs. Wide eyes stared back at her from the surprisingly spotless mirror over the Commodore Grill's bathroom sink. She scrunched her eyes closed, blocking out the dark circles and the exhaustion in her reflection.

She'd driven into Nashville straight from her evening shift. Now she was supposed to look young and fresh-faced. Appealing to an audience who didn't care about the hardships of her life unless they heard about them in a song.

Liz Anne shook her head, slapped some color into her cheeks, then pulled out her eyeliner and lipstick. Bobby wasn't here yet, but she couldn't think about that. Sure, it'd been a relief, thinking she wouldn't be up there alone. And it'd been nice of him to offer. But he was running late, or maybe he'd changed his mind, and at the end of the day, it was all on her.

After one final look in the mirror, Liz Anne stuck the makeup back in her purse, careful not to rumple the good-luck drawing Parker had done for her that afternoon, in between her shifts at the diner. He deserved better than them barely scraping by, and her music was their only chance for a way out of Fairview.

Sounds from the bar's main room grew louder the second she opened the bathroom door, and Liz Anne stalled a moment. People laughing, a singer up on stage, the steady clink of glasses cleaned and filled and toasted and collected… And if she really sucked, it would all fall silent. Uncomfortable. Judging.

Or worse, the place would fill with calls for her to get off the narrow stage stretching along one wall.

You've handled worse. Nearly every time she picked her son up from school. If she could deal with all the "well-meaning" digs, the false concern about Parker's welfare and diet and stitched-up clothing, she could handle two songs here. Just her and her guitar. Which she really should try to tune somewhere out of the way.

She nudged her way to a corner and bent down to pop open the peeling black case.

"Well whadda we got here?"

Liz Anne nearly jumped at the body stepping in close, and she snapped upright. The comeback died on her parted lips in the face of Bobby's grin.

"You all right?" he asked, leaning against the wall.

Surprise knocked some of the nerves out of her. "You're here."

"Where else would I be?" He shot her one of those amused-but-confused looks that she'd begun recognizing as a sign she wasn't behaving like a normal girl in her twenties. A moment later, his head tilted toward the street. "Let's take a walk."

"I've gotta tune my—"

"Bring it." A casual shrug shifted his shoulders.

"What if they call…" She trailed off when the look returned.

"Kane got you this slot. I won't let you miss it."

Right. The normal thing would be to grab her guitar and follow Bobby outside. But she was already trusting him with so much, with her dream—everything she'd been working for.

That he was helping with. She still hadn't figured out why.

Liz Anne exhaled and gripped the neck of her guitar. She followed in Bobby's wake, around the edge of the room. A puff of fresh air hit her as they stepped outside. Bobby led her a ways away from the entrance, then held out his hand for her guitar.

She gave it to him without pause. The instrument she could definitely trust him with. He knew what he was doing, sure, but from the looks of his own guitars, he also had no possible use in the world for her old one. As he tuned, Liz Anne leaned against the cool wall of the Grill, flattening her palms against it so she wouldn't reach into her pocket and check the time on her phone.

"So why're you so jumpy?" Bobby asked, still fiddling with her strings.

"I'm not."

He paused to quirk an eyebrow at her.

She shrugged off the unstated challenge in his expression. "Just nervous, I guess."

He strummed a few more chords before reaching the guitar back out to her. "Liar," he said as she wrapped her fingers below his to take the instrument's weight.

Liz Anne's eyes flew back up to his face. He wasn't pulling on the guitar, but he wasn't letting go, either. "There's just…a lot riding on me. On making this count for something."

"You gotta relax. Enjoy it." He let go of the guitar, and she pulled it close. "You're too young to have the weight of the world on your shoulders."

She nodded, like his words had freed her from her burden. But young or not, she did have an entire world on her shoulders—Parker's.

Bobby pulled back the smile that twitched his lips as Liz Anne thanked the small crowd for listening—which they sort of had—and hurried off the thin raised platform that the Commodore used for a stage. He crossed behind the booker announcing the next singer and stopped in a corner by Liz Anne's side. "That wasn't half bad."

She straightened from tucking her guitar away and pushed her loose hair off of her face. She always kept it down when performing, it seemed. Her eyebrows rose over uncertain eyes.

Bobby shot her a smile. His gaze stalled on the blend of triumph and joy and relief swirling in her expression. He blinked, forcing himself to swallow. "So how're we celebrating?"

Right on cue, her lips popped open to protest.

Bobby's eyes dipped to her mouth, then lower, to the skin modestly showcased by a perfectly reasonable flannel shirt, with just the right number of buttons undone. He hitched his weight onto one leg and knocked the smile up a notch. "C'mon. You did say you'd buy me a beer."

She hesitated still, but gratitude or obligation won out in the end, and she nodded. "One beer."

He snagged them a small, square table. When the waitress came up, Bobby ordered his beer then turned to Liz Anne. "You hungry?" He didn't wait for her to protest before ordering up some chicken strips, onion rings, and sweet potato fries for good measure. She did manage to turn down the sweet tea, switching the order to water. By the time the waitress walked away, Liz Anne looked almost ill, tension puckering her forehead.

"Don't worry." Bobby dropped his hand lightly on hers. "It's on me."

She pulled her hand away, looking a little less green but no more happy. "Why do you keep doing that? This." Her sigh shot out sharply as her head shook. "I really appreciate you helping me," she repeated for the millionth time, "with the guitar, and tonight. But I ain't gonna sleep with you because you helped me out, or paid for some food."

Her anger was overlaid with something else—fear? Helplessness? Bobby leaned back in his chair, fighting the tension in his jaw. Sure, folks might rib him that everything he did was for the sake of getting a girl in bed. Sometimes it was. And there was never a point in bringing up all those times he helped out for no reason at all. So what if Liz Anne thought he was nothing but a creep, trying to pressure her into bed? "Ain't no one keeping you here."

She jolted backward, like she'd expected something different, something more. Then her shoulders straightened and her chin notched up in that defiant way of hers. Hurt flashed in her eyes before her expression fell into her polite version of blank.

Bobby was already kicking himself, and he spoke before she could. "Look,"—he leaned forward but didn't reach toward her—"I don't expect you to sleep with me." He wouldn't have minded—at *all*—but he wasn't exactly running short on options in that department. "I'm helping you out 'cause I can. Nothing more to it." He'd already said more than he usually would. What was it about her that made him want to reach out and explain himself?

But her tension had dropped a tiny bit, and his own shoulders loosened. "Seriously," he continued, relaxing against the back of his chair. "Even if you beg, ain't no way you're getting me in bed."

It took a second, but then her disbelieving chuckle popped the tension between them. "Sorry," Liz Anne said a moment later. "Folks I know aren't exactly nice for no reason." Her gaze switched from him to the waitress setting down their drinks. Bobby tried to swallow, cleared his throat, then reached for his beer.

"Your food'll be right out," the waitress assured before Liz Anne's eyes were back on him.

"Sure you don't want any?" he asked, raising the beer in her direction.

Her lips curved into a sad not-quite-smile. "No, thanks."

Before he could follow up, the food he'd ordered made it to their table. But the dishes only seemed to make Liz Anne more tense. "Hope you'll help me out here," Bobby said.

She started to answer, but then her jaw just shifted uncomfortably. "It's getting late," she finally said.

"Somewhere better to be?" He'd been making a real ass of himself if she had someone waiting for her at home.

"Just gotta be up at seven." Was that a tinge of regret in her voice?

Bobby nodded thoughtfully. "What if I told you, even without my company, these chicken strips are worth five minutes of lost sleep."

Her wry smile echoed his persuasive one. He nudged the plate of chicken closer to her for good measure. She licked her lips, catching the bottom one between her teeth before reaching for a strip, which she dropped on the empty extra plate in front of her. Catching his gaze again, she warned, "Five minutes."

Bobby hooked an onion ring and nodded innocently, repeating after her, "Five minutes."

Seven

*L*iz Anne snaked a sweet potato fry, dipping it into the creamy ranch nestled in the basket as Bobby sipped his beer. She might pay for it tomorrow, but he was right. She could take five minutes, give the guy sitting across from her the benefit of the doubt, and celebrate tonight's more or less successful open mic attempt. And Lord was it a nice break, hanging out as if nothing more important than an early shift waited back home. Not having an empty stomach on the drive back wouldn't hurt, either.

"So tell me something," Bobby said, catching her with a big bite of chicken in her mouth.

Liz Anne raised her eyebrows and tried to balance chewing quickly with not looking gross.

He took another long sip of beer before finishing the thought. "Why is it you don't drink?" Before she could react, he added, "Alcoholic? Mormon?" He paused a beat, a corner of his lips tugging up. "Don't tell me it's 'cause you're counting calories."

Her half-chuckle, half-snort nearly made her choke on the food. She skipped enough meals that *limiting* what she ate for the sake of her looks hadn't been an issue since she'd lost the baby weight. "Wrong on all counts." With her waiting water, she washed down the lingering pieces of breading sticking to her tongue.

He pushed the remaining chicken strips closer to her.

Liz Anne shook her head. She'd had more than enough of his food. "Pretty sure those five minutes are up," she said.

"Not gonna tell me?" Something more intense had replaced the humor of moments ago.

"It's really not that interesting." She'd stopped drinking the moment she found out about Parker. One glass of cheap champagne on her twenty-first birthday, one more on Momma's forty-fifth, but that was it.

Bobby looked disappointed by the answer, and the warmth that had been building between them ebbed away.

Liz Anne fiddled with her napkin until the combination of water droplets and grease from the food tore a hole in it. She sighed. It wasn't like she had anything to be ashamed of, not when it came to abstaining. "Last time I drank, more than a couple sips, I mean… I didn't make the best decisions," she admitted. Having sex with a guy she'd just met against the wall of the old barn where Duke Parnell threw his party wasn't exactly her proudest moment. At least they'd been hidden from view by some empty barrels—or were they haystacks? She shrugged the vague memory away. "*Irresponsible* is the nicest thing you could call it. So now I don't drink."

Bobby didn't respond, just flagged down a waitress and asked her to wrap up the leftover food. "Makes sense," he said then. "If you don't mind giving up another couple minutes of sleep, let me walk you to your car?"

"Sure." She tried to pair it with a smile that wouldn't come. What was he thinking? Obviously, her confession had changed things. Just like her not answering had, only this was worse. For once, Bobby didn't offer a joke or an opinion.

"Betting it's been a while," he said once they'd made it outside. The words twisted Liz Anne's head toward him. He'd exchanged smiles with the waitress, and insisted again he'd pay—not that Liz Anne had fought him all that hard, even if maybe she should've. But otherwise he hadn't said much as they headed out. "Since the last time, and the bad decisions," he explained.

He glanced up and down the street, waiting for her to take the lead, and Liz Anne headed toward her car.

"Not saying you should start drinking, not exactly, but you do seem like you need to relax. Let your hair down. Figuratively," he added at the look she shot him.

"I can't. Not really an option."

"All those responsibilities." He emphasized the last word so it wasn't really a question, but still sounded like one a bit. "Bet you could stand to take a night off," he added, like she was talking about laundry, or dishes—or even work.

She stopped by her car and turned to face him, and he stepped in close. Not close enough to kiss her, or make her uncomfortable, but close enough it had to be on purpose. And if she hadn't needed this to stay simple, only about her music, she might have tilted her chin up so he *could* kiss her.

Because he really did seem *nice*, even if it was only a late-night lie.

Instead, Liz Anne propped her butt against the car, taking some weight off the soles of her feet, which were still annoyed after today's split shifts. "This *was* my night off. And those other times we met up." She shrugged. "That's my time off."

A glimmer of mischief appeared in his eyes. "Seems like someone ought to remind you what it means to relax." He reached around to open her car door. "Making some bad decisions ain't the worst thing in the world."

He stepped aside, but as she set her guitar by the passenger seat, he asked, "What're you so afraid of?"

Where did she even start? Afraid of failing, of never leaving Fairview, of letting Parker down. Of letting someone close enough to hurt her son, or to decide she's worthless, just because she had one. Someone like Bobby couldn't understand that her life wasn't her own anymore, and hadn't been in years. She was always on call, and any wrong decision could end in disaster. She wouldn't do that to Parker.

Silent, Bobby looped the handles of the bag of leftovers around her fingers. She started to reach it back out to him, but he stepped away. As the lit business signs around them flashed colors over his skin, he added, "You drive safe, all right?"

"Okay," she said, swallowing a comment about not needing his charity with the food. It was a stupid thing to pick a fight over, given all the ways he *was* helping her out. "Thanks again, for playing up there with me." That was why they were here— the music.

Bobby's carefree smile slid into place. "Any time."

Eight

"Momma?"

Liz Anne scrunched her eyes against the light. A few beats of silence passed before her mind caught up, and she dragged her eyelids up. "Mmm? Yeah."

"Sorry." She barely heard the quiet apology.

"No, it's okay." Her hand massaged the remnants of sleep away from her face, before she finally woke up enough to find Parker hovering by the door. "You okay?"

He nodded, but frown lines he was way too young for dug into his forehead.

"It's okay, baby." Liz Anne pushed up into a half-sitting position. "I'm just tired. C'mere."

He took a step, hesitated, then ran to her side. She snaked an arm around him and pulled him down onto the bed, snuggling him close and shutting her eyes for another moment. She'd followed up the late night at the Commodore Grill with an extra evening shift Friday, plus her regular double yesterday. There was no way around it: she was beat.

Parker started squirming against her, and after one more moment of quiet, Liz Anne mustered herself into an upright position. He slid off the bed.

"You brush your teeth?" she asked.

"Yep." The solemn, innocent expression was a dead giveaway.

Liz Anne pursed her lips and tilted her head in a gesture that had to be ingrained with all those pregnancy hormones—how often had her own momma looked at her like that? "You sure 'bout that?"

His expression slipped into an impish smile. "No?"

She deepened her disapproval to fight the urge to smile. "Go on," she directed. He scampered out of the room, and Liz Anne closed her eyes for just one more slow breath before shoving herself up to follow him. She brushed one hand through his messy curls as she reached for her own toothbrush. "What do you think," she asked, wetting the bristles, "about heading over to the park today?"

"Can't," he mumbled around the white foam dribbling out of his lips.

"Why not?" She lowered to the edge of the tub and started in on her own teeth.

"It's Kenny's birthday." He rose on tiptoes to spit in the direction of the sink. "His party's s'posed to be in the park. I ain't 'vited."

"Wasn't," she corrected on autopilot. Her toothbrush had stilled, poking out of her mouth as a familiar pang of guilt shot through her. She pulled it out, zeroing in on her son's expression, no longer the least bit sleepy. "Did you want to be invited?"

He shrugged, but a small pout accompanied him wiping his mouth. He was being excluded, all because of her—again. The other mothers were being oh so *Christian* about it all, bullying a little boy.

Liz Anne gulped down the guilt, and anger, and helplessness. "We could still go to the park, if you want. Have a nice little picnic."

He turned to face her, far too serious. "No."

She nodded, the weight of her decisions pressing in on her. But if she hadn't made those choices, she wouldn't have Parker, and that was unimaginable. All she could do now was figure out how to get him away from all the sanctimonious baloney. And meanwhile, she had to make sure Parker had a great day despite it all. She perked up her voice. "Before we do anything else, best get some breakfast in us. You wanna pour us some juice?"

"Yeah." He switched directions instantly, the sadness slipping away at the mention of food. He dropped his toothbrush in the sink and ran out, but Liz Anne didn't have the heart to chastise him. She had a Sunday to save.

Bobby hitched the grocery bags up, balancing them on his hip as he pushed open the door. His mom looked up from her seat at the table, then bent back to her puzzle. Bobby forced some levity into his voice. "Mornin', Ma."

He walked the groceries over to the kitchen and set to putting everything away. His mom was bent over the dining table, still in her dressing gown, fingering cardboard pieces as she tried to put today's image together.

"Mrs. Cotten asked about you at church today," Bobby said, moving between the cupboards and the fridge. "Said she missed seeing you at your book club. Maybe you could make it out next week, see some of your friends." He said it mostly to fill the silence. His mom almost never left the house anymore. Days like today, she didn't even make it to church, but she rarely talked to anyone there now anyway. Her old friends still asked about her when they caught Bobby alone after the service, but nowhere near as often. It was like her life had stopped the moment his dad died.

She still took care of herself, and cooked, and kept the place clean, and all, but it was almost like she expected his dad to come home at any moment, and she had to be there when he did. Or maybe staying in the apartment they'd shared for almost twenty-five years helped her keep him close. Nothing inside their home had changed, either.

Bobby folded up the empty grocery bags then went over to join her at the table. He picked up a puzzle piece, but they'd never been his thing, so he just played with it while she fitted a few more into the rectangular frame.

Once she'd fleshed out a sky-blue corner, he laid one hand on hers. The movement drew her gaze up to him, and she smiled, her eyes clearing. "Robi." She dropped the piece in her fingers and lifted her freed hand to cup his cheek.

"Hi, Mom," he repeated quietly, squeezing the hand he held. He stopped by several times a week to take care of things, but she'd been retreating more and more into the world inside her mind. Days she really saw him were starting to be rare.

She squeezed back, then patted his cheek, saying, "You look hungry." She rocked backward then pushed herself up off the chair. "Let me make you something."

She crossed the ten feet to the kitchen, with a sense of purpose like only feeding him seemed to give her.

Bobby stood to follow her and leaned against a cupboard out of her way. "I was thinking," he said before she pulled open the fridge, "maybe I could take you out to lunch today. There's a great new place nearby I bet you'd love." Of course, "new" was relative.

She clucked her tongue, sounding almost like her normal self. "You know you'll still order fried chicken, and there's no sense in paying someone else to make it for us when I can do that right here." She brought out ingredients automatically as she spoke. After so many years, everything in this kitchen was second nature to her. "You want some mashed potatoes to go with it today?" She was washing them before the question was even finished.

"Sounds great," Bobby said to her back. "Thanks."

As she started in on the chicken, Bobby picked up the potatoes and a peeler. "I took care of Cole's garbage disposal," he told her. "And the right lamps for the upstairs hallway should be in early next week, in case anyone asks." His parents had bought the six-unit building when he'd been a little kid. His dad's life insurance paid off enough of the mortgage that they'd been able to keep the building. Bobby now dealt with any tenant problems, though most times folks did a good job taking care of themselves. Some now even kept tabs on his mom.

It seemed like no time at all before sizzling filled the kitchen. His mom rinsed off her hands and turned toward him, sadness flooding her eyes as it did every time she remembered he couldn't go tell his dad the food was almost ready.

Bobby swallowed down his own lump of grief. "You want me to play you something before we eat?"

She nodded, turning back to the stove to flip the chicken. Bobby went over to the guitar tucked in a corner of the living room, the first one they'd ever bought him. He tweaked the tuning, then warmed up into the freestyle blues his mom loved.

Liz Anne plopped on the couch, curling her neck over the armrest and stretching her legs out. With Parker tucked in bed, she ought to have taken care of their dinner dishes and done a load of laundry, though mostly she wanted to crawl into bed herself.

They'd run around playing a combination of catch and soccer. Then when Momma came home from church, they'd taken the car to the Bellevue Library. Parker was a pretty good reader already, even if that was probably thanks to never being invited anywhere. She really needed to figure out a way to get him some friends—one that didn't require moving. Lord knew that wasn't happening any time soon.

Liz Anne's phone *blipped*, and she pulled it out of her pocket, not opening her eyes until the last moment. The screen showed a simple "Hey" from Bobby.

She hadn't heard from him since Thursday night, not that three days was all that long. Plus she'd been way too busy to think about him in the meanwhile. But something about the simple, un-cheeky text pushed her to respond.

        Liz Anne: Hi

She watched the phone for a while, clutching at the excuse to stay still on the couch. Finally she dropped her hand down. Ten more seconds and she'd make herself go do the dishes. Laundry may have to wait one more day. After the dishes, she'd collapse into bed.

Her phone sounded again right as she'd made herself sit up.

        Good weekend?

She typed, "Busy," then erased it. Was he just asking? Flirting? Gearing up to tell her he was done helping her out for no reason? Something about the messages didn't seem like the usual Bobby. Not that she really knew what was usual for him. They'd only seen each other a handful of times. Even if that was more time than she'd spent with a guy since before Parker was born, it didn't mean anything.

She finally settled on:

> Lots of work. Today was good. Yours?

> Nothing special. You been practicing?

Her lips twitched. She should be grateful he was weirdly invested in teaching her guitar. Or maybe he was just using it as a reason to see her again. Was that possible? He was so nice and carefree… A break from the pressure of her life.

But she needed his help with her music, and she couldn't risk messing that up, even if some part of her wanted something more.

> Not as much as I'd like.

Nine

obby handed Liz Anne a lemonade then leaned back, stretched his legs out, and tilted his beer to his lips. She rolled the chilled bottle between her palms, staring at it like life depended on whether she took a sip. Her guitar case sat unopened by his couch. Rather than pick up his own guitar, Bobby took another long swig of the beer. If he so much as reached for an instrument, she'd spring into "business" mode. Not that he minded teaching her. It wasn't exactly a hardship, and it helped keep his mind off of things with his mom.

Besides, Liz Anne was getting a bit better, more comfortable—with the guitar. He still hadn't figured out how to make her more comfortable with him.

It did seem like he'd found a crack last Thursday, after her open mic slot. Question was whether she'd plastered over it in the last few days.

When she lifted the bottle to her lips, Bobby smiled. He'd picked up the lemonade specially for her, not that she'd welcome knowing that. But like his mom said, good food and drink helped anyone relax. The trouble with Liz Anne was getting her to partake.

After a small sip, she turned to look at him, sighing. "Should we get started?"

Fatigue muted her normal buzz of nervous energy, blurring her sharp edges rather than taking the edge off. "You look like you could use a break more than a lesson," Bobby said. She always had that hint of being a bit too tired. But today, it was flat-out exhaustion.

A plastic smile twisted her face. "I'm fine."

Bobby took a full sip, then set his beer aside and pulled his guitar onto his lap. "You're allowed to be tired, you know," he said, running through an old flamenco-inspired exercise.

Liz Anne's gaze fixated on his fingers, and Bobby switched to a more complicated melody. Not that he was trying to impress her or anything. "Wish I could play like you," she said, her voice somewhere between appreciative and sad.

"Just need more practice."

"And thirty hours in a day." She shook her head, as if she hadn't meant to say it.

"Life keeping you that busy?" He didn't expect much in the way of an answer.

And she proved him right. "You're a good teacher, you know."

"About that." Bobby stopped fiddling around and sat up. "You know we're heading out on tour soon. Leave Thursday." They always did a set of gigs nearby before heading out West.

Her pink lips popped open. "Right." She held his gaze for a drawn-out moment, something glistening in her eyes. "You excited?"

Bobby nodded, still feeling out the odd mood between them tonight. "Ain't nothin' like it."

Her shoulders twitched up a moment, then she leaned over to set down her barely touched lemonade. "Hope you have fun."

She said it like goodbye, and Bobby frowned. "I ain't dying, you know. I will be back."

"Oh, I—" She looked more confused than anything else.

He pulled his frown into a stern teacher look. "And I want you practicing while I'm gone.

She barely cracked a smile.

"All right, seriously. What's eating you today?"

Her eyes widened, and she perked up, her shoulders hitching back like she was heading into battle. "Sorry, uhm—nothing."

Bobby waited.

It didn't take long for Liz Anne's posture to wilt, softening with a small sigh. "Suppose I'm more worn down than I figured. Don't mean to waste your time."

"Does it seem like I mind having you around?"

The question was quiet, serious. Liz Anne dropped her gaze from Bobby's face, to the hands loosely curled around his guitar. The tune he'd played earlier had been so complicated she could barely follow his fingers. And effortless. It would take years for her to even come close, and he'd just been messing around.

Not that she wanted to be a guitarist. She just needed to get somewhere past basic. Good enough to grab attention, maybe even find a manager.

In her silence, Bobby teased a few sounds from his guitar, not quite a melody but a little more than straight chords. As the notes faded, he asked, "So, you going to tell me what's going on?"

What could she say—that she was up by seven every morning to get Parker ready and off to school? And then the rush of her day didn't end until nine at the earliest, almost eleven on days she worked the evening shift. And that was before any singing, writing, or practicing. Every moment was spent working, doing chores, or taking care of Parker. She loved every minute she got with him, but it wasn't exactly relaxing, hanging out with a five-year-old. Her life would be unimaginable to a single guitarist in his twenties, especially one who actually made a living from his music.

So instead of answering, Liz Anne asked, "You play with all sorts of people, right? When you aren't busy with Kane."

A lopsided smile tugged at his lips. "You in the market for a guitarist?"

"If only."

He waited for her to say more.

"But that's what you do, right? Play with…everyone?"

Bobby shrugged and swung his guitar aside to reach for his beer. "Not everyone. But yeah, I've played on a few albums, backing different folk. Perform sometimes, if it doesn't get in the way of things with Kane." When she didn't say anything, he added, "Play at church, too. Why're you asking?"

Liz Anne breathed in slowly, her lungs pressing against the inside of her chest then starting to burn lightly. The breath *whooshed* out before she finally asked, "D'you think I got what it takes?"

Bobby froze, head cocking to the side.

"Be honest, now. You must've seen lots of singers, good, bad, and everything in between. Which one am I?" It didn't make sense, her sudden need for his opinion. He wasn't "somebody," not a talent scout, a manager, a label head—a career maker. But it was also true, even from the background, he'd probably seen tons of folks with dreams, talent even.

Bobby set his beer bottle down by a table leg and resettled on the couch so he was facing her. His solemn expression probably meant the answer was "hell, no." Of course, he was polite enough to say it differently. She shouldn't have asked.

"All right, yeah," he said, and Liz Anne could only blink in response. "I think you've got what it takes." He paused again, his silence thicker even than the Tennessee humidity. "But not yet."

Blankness overwhelmed Liz Anne's mind as her eyes prickled. One more blink, and they were gritty and dry.

"Listen,"—Bobby's hand landed on her knee—"this whole thing here's a process. You need some more time under your belt, time on stage, a few more songs."

Liz Anne's head bobbed up and down, then swayed unevenly from side to side. He hadn't said anything all that bad, or surprising. She passed a hand over her face. She really was worn out.

It would have been nice, though, to have someone other than Parker believe in her. Then again, Parker was more than enough for her. "Thanks," she told Bobby. "No doubt you're right. Sure it's a long road ahead."

"Now c'mon." He leaned back, moving his hand off her leg. "I ain't saying it won't happen. You been writing anything new?"

"Scribbles." Liz Anne picked up the lemonade she'd abandoned, wetting down her mouth to gather herself best she could. "Something wrong with my songs?" she asked, only half teasing. "Besides the guitar parts, I mean."

"I'm no songwriter."

Liz Anne nodded. She'd already asked so much from him, in return for what, one plain old sheet cake? It wasn't fair of her. And she'd come there for a guitar lesson, not career advice.

Ten

How the hell had tonight gotten this serious? Sure, she was there for the sake of her career. But Bobby'd mostly offered to teach her so she could relax when she played, not worry so much about the guitar that she couldn't sing. Then folks would see how good she could be.

Tonight it seemed she was wound so tight just so's not to fall apart. Someone with more to offer might've wrapped his arms around her, pulled her down to snuggle up on the couch. Maybe turned on a dumb TV show they could laugh at together until she fell asleep, which would probably take all of five minutes, looking at her.

But that wasn't Bobby. He liked his co-ed extracurriculars a whole lot more active—and a whole lot more naked. And she'd made it plenty clear she wanted nothing of the sort from him.

So instead he lifted his guitar back onto his lap. "It's all right to take your time, y'know."

New grooves appeared between her eyebrows. "How do you mean?"

"Take it slow, play when you have the time. Why're you wringing yourself dry for this?"

She inhaled sharply. "Ain't you the one who told me not to waste my time if I can't give it my all?"

"I'm just saying, you got your whole life." His fingers stumbled, and Bobby stopped playing again. "You don't got to push yourself like this, working all day then driving out here for a lesson. The music'll be there on your days off."

"I don't get days off," she snapped. The instant apology was written across her face, but she just shook her head gently, like the idea of free time was so ridiculous.

Bobby's jaw shifted, but he managed to hold back on pointing out that maybe that was her problem.

After a long silence when her lips parted and shut several times, she said, "All I'm trying to do is build a better life, okay? Singing's the only way I know how." Her eyes pleaded with him to understand, even as her shoulders inched back into the ramrod-straight posture she used like a shield.

"Well, then. Can I make a suggestion?" There actually was one thing he'd been thinking about when it came to her songs, not that it was really his place to say.

Relief painted over her expression, and she exhaled harshly, her chest falling and rising visibly before her breathing settled back into normal.

"All right, well. Let me get another beer first. You want anything?" he asked, getting off the couch.

She didn't bother declining, her head shaking on autopilot. But by the time he closed the fridge, she'd picked up the lemonade again. So that was something.

Liz Anne took another small sip as Bobby tossed back half a bottle of beer. Obviously whatever he wanted to tell her, it wasn't good. His faint scowl wasn't helping, but she could take it. Even with fatigue vibrating through every bit of her, threatening to tear her apart. She was there to get any help she could.

"I've been thinking a bit, 'bout your songs," he said, and Liz Anne zeroed in on his face. "That one quiet one we've been working on, it ain't bad. But the others…" He paused, his frown etching deeper around his mouth. "It almost feels like they aren't yours."

What was he implying? "I wrote all my songs," she protested.

"No, I know that. I ain't saying you didn't write them." He paused. "But when you sing them, it's like karaoke. Like you wrote what you think you're supposed to, but it doesn't ring true for you."

The pit in her stomach yawned larger. Her songs were supposed to be normal, a regular twenty-something girl's life— hanging out in bars, casual relationships, all the fun stuff she'd never really experienced. No one wanted to hear about changing diapers or parent–teacher meetings.

"All's I'm saying is, folks aren't going to connect to your music if even you don't. You gotta write true."

"People don't want to hear the truth."

Bobby's lips slanted up briefly, almost like he understood.

Wishful thinking.

"No, not always," he agreed. "Genuine's the better word. Take that bar song." He downed some more beer then pulled his guitar into position. "The chorus is good, but the rest, well…" He played a quick intro, then half-sang her words, "Without you, I'm still flying. I'll make it through, won't see me crying." He kept playing, but stopped singing to ask, "Is that really about some guy, flirting in a bar? The rest of the song sounds like you're trying to copy someone, something else."

His fingers stopped echoing her melody, and Liz Anne swallowed down the lump in her throat. Did everyone see through her like this? "And the other one?" she asked. He'd only heard three of her songs: one okay, one bad, and the last?

Bobby sighed. "Feels young, defensive. But like you want it to be strong, kicking butt and taking names… And it just ain't there."

Liz Anne nodded, the pit inside her now threatening to swallow her up. Kane had told her she wasn't ready, her songs weren't good enough, that very first day. Why hadn't she listened?

And Bobby didn't owe her anything, but still—the anger, the *shame* that burned through her. He'd dutifully helped her with the guitar part, and all the while, he knew the songs weren't good enough. Would never be good enough. And these were the best ones she had. She was fooling herself, thinking she'd ever get anywhere singing, that she could ever give Parker the life he deserved.

"Hey." Bobby's hand landed on her shoulder. Concern or maybe pity drew his eyebrows down over his hazel eyes.

Try as she might, Liz Anne couldn't force a smile. "Thanks, for the feedback," she forced out.

"I told you," he said, his kindness eating away at her, "I ain't a songwriter. But you wrote that first song too, the good one. So you can do it." His hand dropped away. "You just can't be so afraid of showing people who you are."

Liz Anne nodded again. Problem was, she was nobody, other than Parker's mom, and that girl who got pregnant in high school. Neither made for a good song.

Bobby was looking at her like he wanted an answer. But there wasn't one he'd want to hear.

Disappointment filled his eyes, and he resettled on the couch so they were farther apart, not quite touching distance. No more space between them than usual, but it felt bigger.

"Who's your favorite singer?" he asked, switching back into teacher mode.

Liz Anne took a deep breath and tried to match his nonchalance. "You waiting on me to say Kane?"

A quick grin flashed her way. "Let's take him out of the running."

"Miranda Lambert, for one. She's…incredible." Of course, the South was littered with girls who wanted to be Miranda

Lambert. Not that Liz Anne wanted to *be* her. But a fraction as successful would be nice.

Bobby's eyes widened at the name, but he tried to hide the skepticism. "Okay, all right." He nodded like he was thinking, staring down at the guitar still in his lap. It looked so natural there, in a way her instrument never felt.

"A great example, actually," Bobby said after a moment. "Whatever she wants to say, she finds a way to do it in a way people connect to, can relate. She doesn't hide behind country music, she makes it fit her. Her voice, her message. That's what you gotta do."

"Oh, is that all?" The sarcasm slipped out. Could she blame it on the fatigue again?

Bobby's small smile grew into something bigger, appreciative. "So there is some personality under all that…" The humor slipped into an odd heat that disappeared when he blinked. "Stress."

Warmth filled Liz Anne's cheeks. That had to be the fatigue, too. For that matter, she probably ought to get going. Even if she hadn't yet touched her guitar tonight. "It's getting late," she said quietly.

"Yep." His gaze lingered on her, before something snapped him out of the appraisal. He set his guitar in the armchair beside the couch and stood. "You want to stay here, just"—he cut off her objections with a small gesture—"to get some sleep before driving?"

It almost sounded smart, not getting behind the wheel while she could barely keep herself upright.

"You'd have to get up a bit earlier for work, is all. I'd even give you the choice of bed or couch." A bit of the normal Bobby humor had worked itself back into his expression. And yet, he stood back, thumbs tucked into his pockets. Completely non-threatening, and not at all interested.

How tempting was it to just pass out, right here on his couch? More than comfortable enough for a few hours' sleep.

But if Parker woke up in the middle of the night and she wasn't there…

Liz Anne shook her head. "Nice of you to offer, but, I really ought to be getting home."

"All right. Well," he said as she gathered up her things, "do-over for this lesson tomorrow?"

Nearly at the door, she turned to face him. She worked split shifts on Wednesdays. Eleven wasn't too late for Bobby, but she'd be dead on her feet. Maybe even worse than tonight, so what was the point? "I just can't," she said. How was it he was doing her a favor, and she was the one turning him down?

Bobby didn't seem all that bothered. He just shifted behind her to hold the door open. "Then I'll want hear some new songs when I get back."

"You giving me homework, now?" But something about the expectation, the belief maybe she *could* write something good… That or maybe standing so near to him was melting the edges of that inner pit, filling the hole with oozing lava.

Bobby swallowed and took a small step back. "You let me know you got home safe, all right?"

Liz Anne took the cue to step out, though the night air was hardly cool enough to help. "Hope the tour goes good," she said before walking to the car.

She would have taken a minute or two to pull herself together behind the wheel, but Bobby stood in the doorway, watching until she drove away.

Eleven

"Who died?" Bobby asked, sliding into his seat for a late breakfast Sunday morning. Kane and Mitch were already sipping coffees, looking far too grim for how their first couple of nights out had gone.

Steve came out of the back of the little diner and took the last spot in their booth. His face didn't give anything way, or maybe he didn't know what was happening either. Impossible to tell with the stoic drummer.

"We need to decide something, soon," Mitch said, looking at Kane, who frowned, then pulled out his phone and started scrolling through the contacts.

Bobby looked across the table at the manager and Steve, who calmly picked up his coffee.

"Let's start with the problem," Bobby suggested. "How bad can it be before breakfast?"

No one cracked a smile.

"The Fortners are out," Kane said.

"What happened?" Steve asked.

Bobby flipped open the menu. The Fortner sisters were good, promising, and they'd played well the last couple of nights. But this wasn't something Bobby could help with, so he might as well find something to eat.

"Family emergency, didn't say what," Mitch explained. "I'll have a card for you to sign later." His phone chimed, and he flipped it over to read the screen, saying, "We can get Alicia Mae out, starting Thursday, but that still leaves tonight."

"So are we adding back some songs?" Steve asked.

Bobby let the plastic-covered menu fall back to the table-top. If they were changing their set, he actually had to pay attention.

Mitch was frowning down into his phone now, but Kane had given up the search. "It's that or find someone else, some-one with a decent sound, right feel, in the next couple hours," Kane said.

They all paused the shoptalk as a waitress came by. Bobby shot her a lazy smile, and she blushed, smiling back as she refilled his coffee. Mitch cleared his throat, making her jolt with a soft, "Right." She topped off the others' mugs then pulled out her pad.

Once she'd gotten their orders down, Steve asked, "What's wrong with reprising some of the older songs?"

"Step backward," Mitch said right as Kane said, "Nothing."

Steve glanced between them then met Bobby's gaze, his eyebrows popping up with a "they're fighting already" look.

"Why're we making this such a big deal?" Bobby asked. How many times had they played without an opener? Damn near all of them, except these last few nights.

"Perception. Expectations." Mitch set down the phone. "People know the Fortners are supposed to be there, it's on all the promotional materials, the website. Fans are looking forward to it, plus it looks good, passing along goodwill to newer artists."

Kane didn't seem convinced, and Steve, as always, stayed out of it, stirring some cream into his coffee.

"You telling me people coming tonight won't be happy to hear some extra songs?" Kane asked.

Plus they could vamp for a bit, add a little chitchat. The girls coming to see them mostly wanted Kane—the music was kind of a lucky bonus.

"And who'd want to drive all the way out for one show?" Kane added.

"Maybe the club knows some locals, someone vetted," Mitch said.

These two were making mountains out of the tiniest of molehills. Hell, Bobby could probably strum a couple covers if they were that desperate for an opener. "Hey," he interrupted, a great idea hitting him now that the caffeine'd kicked in. "What about Liz Anne?"

That got everyone's attention, but they weren't exactly jumping on board.

"I've been working with her," Bobby reminded. "And she's really getting better."

"'Better' ain't *good*," Mitch grumbled.

Bobby scowled at him and focused on Kane. "She did that open mic spot, went pretty well. And she's only a couple hours' drive away."

Kane didn't shoot him down, but he wasn't agreeing, either.

"It ain't a big deal for us either way, but it'd sure mean a lot to her." Bobby turned back to Mitch. "And what was that about helping newer artists?"

"She have the songs?" Kane asked.

Bobby shrugged, then grinned. "Better than last time."

The other three men exchanged some looks, but ultimately it was going to be Kane's call. Sure enough, he fixed Bobby with a warning look, like Liz Anne had better live up to Bobby's description. But she would.

"Okay," Kane agreed with a small nod. "Let's call her."

Liz Anne scratched out another old line, then dropped the pencil onto her notebook to play through the reworked second half of the verse. *But then you walked away and nothing stayed the same, I hear 'em whispering. But without you...*

She palmed the vibrating strings, biting down on her lip to stop from smiling. The new version seemed like it was working. Still leaning toward normal country, but with a little bit more of her worked in, like Bobby'd said. And no one knew what it was like to live in a gossipy town like she did. She just needed one more verse, and this song might actually be done. Well, again. Re-done.

Liz Anne shook her head then reached for her glass of strawberry lemonade. Which was empty.

She set aside the guitar and headed to the kitchen, pausing at the table to look over Parker's shoulder at his drawing. A human-horse mix was battling something that was probably supposed to be a dragon, but colored like a tiger. He was just finishing up drawing the stripes through the round wings. Instead of distracting him, Liz Anne moved on to the fridge.

As she poured them both some more lemonade, Parker said, "Momma?"

"Yeah, baby. You all done with your drawing?" She tucked the pitcher back on its shelf, then brought his cup over.

"Yep." He pushed the sheet of paper away. "You all done with your song?" he echoed.

"No, can't say I am." She twisted the drawing toward her, but she didn't miss Parker's small pout. She might be on a roll, but he was only five. She couldn't ask him to keep himself occupied much longer. Maybe if they had lunch first, she could get another half hour after.

"What do you say we both take a break?" she suggested. "Have a little something to eat."

Instantly his face brightened. "Yeah. Pancakes?"

Liz Anne laughed. "How about sandwiches? Or maybe we could whip up some spaghetti and hot dogs."

Parker slipped off his chair and headed to the cupboards. "Spaghetti," he announced.

Liz Anne's phone rang, and she slipped it out of her pocket. "You wait for me to get that water boiling," she instructed before looking at the screen.

Which said Kane Hartridge's manager was calling. Liz Anne's heart started pounding, but it had to be a wrong number. An accident. Still, it would be rude not to answer. "Hello?"

"Liz Anne, it's Mitch Dennings here." So, probably not a misdial.

"How are you, Mr. Dennings?" she asked, taking a few steps away from the kitchen where Parker clanged an empty pot onto the counter.

"We found ourselves in a bit of a situation here, for the show tonight. Bobby mentioned you might be able to help us out."

"Tonight?" Liz Anne's eyes found her son, waiting patiently as ever for his lunch. She walked over to the pantry to find him something that would suit as a snack for now.

"If you can make it out here, to take the place of the opener," the manager said.

Was he really offering her another chance to open for Kane Hartridge? Had Bobby talked them into it for some reason? Dennings hadn't actually said what happened to the opener they'd chosen… Or had she missed it?

"'Fraid we can't pay you more than a bit of gas money and a couple of drinks. But we'd appreciate you helping us out at the last minute like this, if you're able."

"Oh, well…" Would saying yes make her a terrible mother? Sundays were their only full day together, and she'd have to take the car, leaving Parker stuck at home with her momma. If Momma agreed to it at all. "I'd have to make arrangements, take care of some things. Could I call you back, let you know?"

"I understand, but we need an answer real soon. It'd take you or anyone time to get here. Can you let me know in the next half hour?"

Parker appeared at her side, staring up at her. If he said no, she'd stay home with him. That'd be the right thing to do, wouldn't it? "Yes, sir, I will," she told the manager. "Thank you for thinking of me."

"What's wrong, Momma?" Parker asked in a small voice when she hung up.

"Nothing's wrong, baby." Liz Anne handed him a packet of fruit snacks and set her hand on his shoulder to guide him back to the table so they could talk.

He tore open the packaging as Liz Anne fought another wave of guilt.

"Listen, Parker."

He paused with a smushed purple snack piece partway to his mouth, his round eyes meeting hers.

"That was Mr. Dennings, the manager for that singer I told you about. The one I got to play with a couple weeks ago."

The snack was quickly popped into his mouth and shoved toward one side, bulging out his cheek. "Does he want to make you famous?"

A chuckle bubbled out of her mouth, and Liz Anne nudged Parker's glass toward him. "Not quite. Don't forget to chew." She took a deep breath as he gulped down a couple more of the fruit snacks. "He did ask if I could open for Mr. Hartridge tonight."

Parker drained half his lemonade, the glass clunking on the table when he set it down. "Tonight?"

"Yep. But it'd mean I have to leave, right after lunch. I know we normally hang out on Sundays, so I won't go if you don't want me to. But it'd be a pretty big opportunity."

"Can I come?"

"Oh, I wish." She reached out to curl her fingers around his small hand. "It's a couple hours away, and I won't be playing 'til really late. And it's a school night." A thought struck her as Parker's frown deepened into a pout. How late did their gigs go? How much sleep would she be able to get before needing to get Parker off to school like normal? Lizane sighed, squeezing his hand gently. "Actually, baby, I might not be able to take you to school tomorrow, so grandma would take you."

Parker pulled his hand from hers, his gaze now trained somewhere on the floor between them.

Liz Anne let the silence stretch between them so Parker could have time to think. She could practically hear the seconds tick by, but there was no way she was flipping her phone over to look at the time. Even if Mr. Dennings did need an answer ASAP.

"Should I call grandma?" she prodded. "Talk to her?"

He didn't answer, or move. Not even to pick up the remaining fruit snacks.

"Parker."

"Why can't I come?"

"I just told you why. It's a school night. And I probably won't be playing until way past your bedtime." She slipped off the chair to crouch in his line of sight. "You know I want you there, baby. But it's more important for you to get a good night's sleep, and you have school in the morning. And I will do everything I can to come back as early as I can, okay? And I'd definitely still pick you up."

He sighed, the heavy drop in his shoulders tearing at her heart. "Promise?" he asked in that small voice that ate away at her insides.

Her breath caught on her exhale. "Promise." She stood and wrapped an arm around her son, tugging him in for a hug. He leaned into her waist for a moment, then pulled away to reach for his snack. Liz Anne smiled, shaking her head, and asked, "What do you say we get lunch started while I call grandma?"

Twelve

obby nodded at Liz Anne as she came up to his seat at the bar. Like the first time she'd played with them, she was vibrating with tension, the stress bracketing around her lips. And if he wasn't wrong, she was holding back tears.

Bobby slipped from the stool. She definitely hadn't been this upset, or nervous, when she'd gotten there, right around their sound check. And she'd mostly been scribbling away in an old notebook since. This was one of the places that had a green room for artists, even if it was tiny. As soon as she was done with the small salad she'd ordered in place of dinner, Liz Anne had curled up in a corner of the old loveseat crammed against one wall.

Bobby'd thought about interrupting her, but he didn't want the others to make all the wrong assumptions. "You doing all right?" he asked her now.

She hesitated, staring at him like a rabbit frozen in the head-lights. "Listen," she started, "I know you don't owe me nothing. And I'm so grateful you got Mr. Dennings to call me for tonight. But I'd pay you back for it, or get you another—"

"Hold on." Bobby cupped her shoulders. "What in the world are you talking about?"

She shuddered with her exhale. "I was fiddling with my guitar, and one of the strings sounded off, so I was trying to get it tuned right, and…"

"You popped a string," Bobby finished for her, the worry that had been coiling in his gut melting away.

"Yes." She glanced at one of his hands and took a step back, out of reach.

Bobby tucked his thumbs into his pockets.

"Do–do you have an extra B string I could use? I promise to replace it." She looked desperate, like he was a loan shark and she was up to her ears in debt. And her eyes were definitely red from holding back tears.

But handing her the backup string lying in his case might not be the right way to go. For one thing, new strings needed to be broken in. He could lend her his guitar, but really, this seemed like an opportunity. She sounded so much better when she sang without worrying about what her hands were doing. "Nah, I don't, sorry."

She paled, her eyes darting around, her breath coming out in short puffs.

"But I could play with you," he added quickly. "If you want."

"What?" Her eyes found him again. "Won't Kane mind?"

Bobby's lips edged up. "Think he'll be okay with sharing. And I do know all of your songs," he reminded.

Some of the stress seemed to seep out of her stance, but then she took a half-step back, shaking her head. "I took your advice." She tried to smile. "I was going to play something different, hopefully better."

Well, shoot. He hadn't seen that one coming. "You wrote new songs that quick?"

"Just one, really. It probably ain't any good. For 'Without You,' I just switched up some of the words." She shrugged, tucking her thumbs into her pockets. "Figured I could play 'From My Lips' still, but I guess it don't much matter now."

"Well, hold on." Bobby's hand reached out, but he dropped it without touching her. "That's two of your songs I definitely know. Maybe you could do a cover of something for a third. Something you relate to."

She started protesting before he'd finished the thought. But Mitch paused beside them with a simple, "Problem?" Liz Anne's lips clamped shut.

"Nope," Bobby said, still keeping her gaze.

Mitch nodded and kept on moving toward the green room, or maybe the booker's office.

"Not a fan of singing covers?" Bobby prompted. He stepped back, leaning his elbows on the bar behind him.

Liz Anne's jaw shifted, and the muscles in her neck twitched as she swallowed. Then her weight dropped into one hip. "Don't know anything well enough to get up there with tonight." She paused, glancing around them at the nearly empty bar. "Maybe this wasn't such a good idea." Her eyes met his once more. "And it ain't your problem. I should tell Mr. Dennings."

Bobby frowned, standing straight, then caught himself and sank back down onto a barstool. No point in letting this seem as life-and-death as she was making it. "How's about a hymn? I know you know those well enough." He dropped his brows into a mock scowl. "Unless you're a complete heathen."

The tension hovered between them for a beat, but then a breathless chuckle escaped her. "Spent my fair share of time in church."

"What'll it be, then? 'Standing on the Promises'? 'Just a Closer Walk.'" Though then folks might think she was copying Miss Patsy Kline.

Steve crossed behind Liz Anne, heading the same direction as Mitch had gone. Bobby paused in thinking up song possibilities to call, "Steve!" He held his hand up. "Keys?"

Steve pulled the bus's keys from his pocket and tossed them over.

Bobby looked back to Liz Anne. "Should I be getting my guitar?"

She frowned, a little crinkle appearing on her forehead as she obviously tried to figure out what was in it for him, what she might owe. Her mental math was way more complicated than any Bobby cared to do.

Finally she nodded, lips pressing into a flattened line before she forced out, "Thank you."

Bobby smiled, shaking his head a bit at how hard she made everything. "You bet."

"Without you, better off now," Liz Anne sang, throwing a glance over her shoulder at Bobby. He faded the melody line out as she wrapped up the last snippets of lyrics, looking over the heads of folks in the club. "Oh I'm free, free without you."

Applause filtered in over the last lines, and there was even a shouted "yeah!" tossed her way at the end of the song.

Liz Anne grinned, her heart battering against her rib cage. This was actually going okay. "Thank you," she murmured into the mic.

She glanced at Bobby again, who met her gaze this time with a knowing smile of his own. With a small breath, she planted her palms flat on her hips so she wouldn't pick at her nails. Hard as it was to put her own music out there, this next song might be even harder.

"It's such an honor to sing for all y'all here tonight. This last song, well,"—she widened her smile, aiming for charming to cover up the nerves—"I haven't sung it in a good long while. But it's sure to be familiar to many of you. And I just hope to do it justice."

She stepped back from the mic as Bobby strummed a simple three-count intro. She'd half-expected him not to know this one, but he hadn't been kidding about playing at his church.

"I come to the garden alone," Liz Anne began, the words scratching out of her throat. It had been her favorite hymn once, before she'd stopped being welcome in church. But she could sing here. "While the dew is still on the roses…"

The room had hushed, eyes turning toward her. Then again, folks were pretty much trained to listen respectfully to hymns. Liz Anne's fingers clenched into fists, but then she let them shake loose and stepped closer to the mic, one hand coming to rest on it for the chorus. "And He walks with me, and He talks with me." Her face lifted to the mic as her eyes closed. "And He tells me I am his own… And the joy,"—her eyes opened to meet the gazes of those listening—"we share, as we tarry there, none other has ever known."

Even Kane, lingering toward the side of the room by the bar, seemed to be smiling as she sang the second verse. Steve stood beside him, looking like he couldn't quite figure Liz Anne out. Of course, she wasn't so hard to figure—just another country girl with an okay voice and a big ol' dream. Give or take a five-year-old kid.

She led into the second chorus, her head twisting to catch Bobby's smile as he joined in. He faded back out on the last line, leaving the third verse to her. But there his voice was again on the last chorus.

And his singing seemed to encourage those listening to join in as well, genuinely broadening Liz Anne's smile. A sheen even came to her eyes. She'd missed singing with others like this. They'd kicked her out of the church choir the minute she'd started to show with Parker.

At the end of the chorus, Bobby led into the repeat couple lines, the room hushing once more. But instead of the standard echo of the last two chorus lines, Liz Anne's favorite lines popped out. "And the melody that He gave to me, within my heart is ringing."

There was a beat of silence, but then applause filtered in, people smiling at her as it ramped up for a second. Liz Anne dropped her hand from the mic, taking it all in. Her brain kicked in, and she said, "Thank you. That was such a pleasure, and I know our night's just getting started. Who's excited to hear the fantastic Kane Hartridge?" Cheers filled the space before she'd even finished his name.

Kane stepped up on the little raised stage. Liz Anne backed away from the mic, but as he reached the center of the stage, he turned partly to gesture to her. "Let's show some appreciation for this girl right here." He nodded at her, then turned back to the room.

Liz Anne took that as her cue, lifting a hand to the room as she crossed behind Kane. He added, "And I hear her guitarist isn't half-bad." That got a chuckle from folks who knew Bobby played with Kane.

Smiling herself, Liz Anne ducked into the small backstage room that held her bag and guitar. Her heart still pounded from the adrenaline of being up there. Here, in private, she could admit: that had actually gone *well*.

✧ ✧ ✧

Bobby pushed open the green room's door as it swung shut behind Liz Anne. Her eyes jumped to catch his gaze, the light flush on her face adding a touch of life and stopping him in his tracks. "Nice job out there," he managed to say.

"Thanks again." Her voice was a bit breathy. With the excitement of singing, of course.

She'd stepped out of the way of the door, but in the tiny room, that still left her in arm's reach. Bobby moved forward so the door could shut, bringing them even closer. He was there to grab his bass, but the way Liz Anne was looking at him…

With anyone else, the invitation would have been clear. Still, Bobby took the couple steps away to switch out his guitar for his bass. When he turned back around, she'd pivoted to face him.

"Really. Thanks, for that tonight," she said, voice quiet, or maybe a little hoarse.

Shallow breaths nudged her chest up and down. She swept the hair back off her shoulder. Her chin tilted up to him. Bobby shifted forward, his eyebrows lifting in question, or maybe challenge. He couldn't be the only one feeling the heat between them right then.

Her eyes dropped to his lips, and for a heartbeat he was sure she'd chicken out, back away.

But then her mouth met his, lightly, barely pressing their lips together. Bobby dipped his head, closing the remaining distance between them so he could kiss her properly. Her hand came up to his shoulder, her lips parting for him. His free hand cupped her head, fingers sliding into the silkiness of her hair.

Strings pressed into his other hand as it clenched around the bass's neck, and Bobby pulled back, brushing her lips one more time before lifting away. She dropped back down from her toes, questions in her eyes, lips red from their kiss.

But this was so not the time for this.

As if Bobby'd forgotten, Mitch called his name through the door.

He had to get back on stage. As a singer, she had to understand. "Hope you're sticking around awhile," he told her, before rushing out the door.

<h1 style="text-align:center">Thirteen</h1>

She shouldn't have done that, kissing Bobby. Letting him kiss her. What had gotten into her?

The music.

All those nerves from earlier, jangling through her, and things had actually gone okay up on stage. And just about all of that was because of Bobby.

And that kiss…

Her lips couldn't actually still be tingling, could they?

She stroked a finger over her bottom lip, to brush the feeling away or maybe to keep it close.

Shaking her head, Liz Anne double-checked her things were squared away, then made her way back out and over to an empty spot by the bar. She'd have to get going soon to make it home, but she could still take a few minutes to enjoy some of Kane's music.

Bobby was back in his spot on the stage, fingers flying over his bass. He grinned over at some girls flashing their own flirty smiles, and Liz Anne turned away, twisting more toward the bar itself.

A beer appeared beside her, hovering for her to take it. Before she could turn it down, her eyes caught Mr. Dennings' face. She curled her fingers around the bottle, notching up her own smile.

"Not bad up there tonight," he said, then tipped his drink to his lips.

Liz Anne exhaled, shaking off her weird mood. The music was what mattered. "Thank you."

"Know you have a bit of a drive ahead of you, but some folks might want to chat with you during the set break." He took a longer sip, nearly draining his glass. "And there's always room on the bus."

Liz Anne's face froze along with any response. Sure, staying might be good for her music—or maybe bad, spending the night on a bus with all the others—but it didn't matter. Parker had to get to school in the morning, and her momma needed the car to get to work. But she couldn't just stare at Kane's manager like an idiot. She lifted the beer to her lips, plugging the bottle with her tongue so she wasn't drinking more than a couple drops.

Dennings' eyes stayed on her a moment. Then he tilted his glass to her and moved on toward a cluster of women near the other end of the bar, just as Kane said something on stage about folks buying a round for anyone without a drink.

Liz Anne rolled the chilled bottle between her palms. She sat back more fully on her stool, then set the beer on the bar. Better she stick with water, which she'd grab when the bartender freed up. And meantime, she could enjoy the music.

It didn't take long for her to get swept along with the rest of the audience, laughing at Kane's jokes and even tapping her foot in the air a few times.

She startled when he announced they'd be taking a short break. How had it gotten to be so late?

But maybe it was a good thing. Now she could say a quick thank you and goodbye. She'd just have to catch him before his fans swallowed them in their ranks.

Liz Anne slid off the barstool, then grabbed the beer. She could at least pretend to fit in with the crowd enjoying their night.

She caught up to Kane and the others only a few steps away from the stage. Bobby's eyebrows lifted at the bottle she held, but she needed to say her piece to Kane so he wouldn't think she was rude for leaving during their next set.

"Not bad tonight," Kane said, stretching a hand out toward Liz Anne.

Bobby smiled. She'd sounded good tonight, more connected. Maybe now the others would see the potential in her that he had.

"Thank you," Liz Anne breathed, shaking Kane's hand.

Kane took a moment to sign an autograph and grab a quick picture with a girl showing off everything she had in a tight tank top and mini skirt.

Bobby didn't miss the slight roll of Liz Anne's eyes. She was flushed, rosiness filling her cheeks. But she also looked a might happier than usual.

As the fan stepped away to giggle with her friends, Kane turned back to Liz Anne. "Listen," he said, "we always do something on Memorial Day. A nice barbecue for friends and family, people in the community. You should come, play a little something."

Liz Anne's mouth popped open, the surprise of the offer wiping away her smile.

"Bring your family," Kane added. A new group of fans approached them, reaching out drinks to Kane and Bobby.

Bobby ramped up the charm, thanking the girl who'd handed him a beer, and a napkin with her number. They caught a quick selfie as Kane told Liz Anne, "We'll talk details later."

He disappeared into the crowd, and Liz Anne called "thank you" his way. She blinked at the floor with a small smile, shoulders shrugging.

Memorial Day was always a good time, getting folks together at Kane's with a big barbecue, everyone's families. Last couple of times, Bobby'd invited some of their tenants along, too. It was great, seeing the families, the kids running around. Hopefully his mom would be up for some socializing. And playing for a friendly crowd in a good mood was always fun.

Having Liz Anne there would be good, too. Hell, maybe she'd finally have some fun off the stage.

She met Bobby's eyes, hers glinting with hope or maybe happiness. She hesitated a moment, then gestured over her shoulder with the beer bottle. "I better get going on home."

"You been drinking?" he asked.

She chuckled, shaking her head like it was the most ridiculous thing he could have said. "No." She held out the bottle toward him. "You want it?"

"I'm all right." Though his throat was feeling a little dry. Still, ignoring his own beer, he said, "Walk you out?"

That hint of heat started building between them, and Bobby's fingers tightened against the cold moisture of the beer bottle.

"Sure," Liz Anne mouthed. Or probably said, but he couldn't quite hear her over the chatter. They started toward the green room, Bobby following as Liz Anne picked her way around the clusters of people.

"Bobby!" Steve called from the center of the room.

Liz Anne's head jerked toward the sound, then she smoothly turned back around to face him. "Go," she said, nodding. Before Bobby could say anything, she added, "I'll see you 'round."

"Count on it," Bobby said, then got on back to work, heading toward Steve's crowd.

Fourteen

*L*iz Anne leaned closer to the mirror and patted a fresh layer of concealer under her eyes. She must've lost her mind, agreeing to Bobby coming by tonight after Parker was asleep. But her momma had plans for once, which also meant she had the car. And maybe it was better Liz Anne saw Bobby sooner rather than later, figure out if they could move on with the guitar lessons without that kiss getting in the way.

With one more look in the mirror, Liz Anne twisted her ponytail into a quick bun then shut off the light. She checked in on Parker, sleeping with his arm curled around an old Curious George doll she'd gotten him for his second birthday. She checked the nightlight, then shut the door softly.

Her fingers drummed on her thighs as she made sure the brownies were still where she'd left them on the kitchen counter, and the pitcher of tea was full in the fridge.

She straightened the quilt covering up the worn patches on their old couch, then circled the room again, making sure there wasn't anything too old, too broken, or too stained that she'd missed. Money was tight, but that fact didn't have to jump out and slap Bobby in the face the moment he got there.

Was he running late?

She pulled out her phone to check the time. Still only eight forty-five. Fifteen minutes at least before he'd show up.

If he showed up. Would he think it was too awkward? She scrolled over to their text messages from earlier. *Free tom?* he'd written last night, the words now staring back at her from the screen.

Liz Anne shook her head and set the phone, screen-side down, on one end of the couch. She picked up her guitar and settled on the other end to run through some quiet exercises. At least she'd managed to pick up a new string yesterday.

Just a few seconds in, her fingers tripped up on the strings, and Liz Anne stopped, shutting her eyes. What was wrong with her tonight? Nerves fluttered through her hands, her fingers, almost as bad as when she was onstage. But those times, the audience seemed to help out, take a bit of that energy into the bodies surrounding her. Tonight was something different.

She nearly jumped when a knock came at the door.

Bobby bit back a grin when Liz Anne opened the door. She was pulled so tight, if she'd have been a string, she would have snapped. Even her hair was pulled back, almost invisible.

She probably thought it made her look more serious, or more strict. Really, it made her eyes look bigger, her lips plumper. She stepped back from the door, and Bobby took a couple steps inside. Her place was nice, if a little worn down.

"Get you something?" she asked, shutting the door.

"I'm good." Bobby made his way over to the couch and leaned his case against it.

"I could get you some sweet tea, or a brownie." She hovered where he'd left her, like this wasn't her home to begin with.

"What's going on with you?"

She exhaled and made her way to the kitchen, like she'd only then remembered how to move. "You 'bout to tell me I look tired again?"

She had him there. Maybe he'd mentioned it one time too many. "Nope," he said as she poured a glass of tea. "You look pretty great from where I'm standing."

She froze again, pitcher hovering in the air. Bobby grinned at her back. She was driving herself crazy about that kiss. And hell, if she didn't want a repeat, he'd deal with it. But they definitely couldn't go on like this.

With rigidly controlled movements, she opened the fridge, slid the pitcher onto a shelf, and firmly shut the door. Bobby walked up behind her.

She turned around, saw him, and just about jumped out of her skin. The surprise sent her chest into a rapid rise and fall beneath the faded gray tee shirt with an old-school helmet on it. She tried to cover, though, hitching her weight into one hip and tucking her thumbs into the back pockets of her jeans. Course, all that really did was push her chest up toward him.

Bobby met the challenge, holding her gaze straight on.

She wavered first, like he'd known she would. Her eyes dropped down, then further, before she looked back up at him. "What're we doing here?" she asked, a hint of a smile edging her words. Or maybe it was exasperation.

"Well I don't know what you're doing," Bobby said and took a step forward. "But I'm about to kiss you."

Her hands dropped down by her sides, her eyes widening.

Bobby set his hands on her waist, his thumbs brushing up her sides. "If you'll let me," he added.

For a moment it seemed like maybe she'd say no, step away. But then she took her own small step forward, tilting her face up toward him. Bobby smiled, then their lips met.

Liz Anne ran the water in the sink and passed her fingers through the stream as it disappeared.

What am I doing?

Sure, she'd hooked up a few times over the years. In the back of a truck, sometimes a booth at the diner if she was the one locking up. Always a one-time thing when someone caught her eye and she had the minutes to spare.

But never at home.

Now Bobby was sitting on her couch, playing something or other she could hear through the bathroom door. That same ease of his playing filled every move of his hands, his lips, his body pressing against hers, coaxing pleasure. Tingling through parts of her he hadn't even touched.

Her fingers slipped up into her bun, working the four pins loose before pulling out the elastic tie. Her hair coiled down over her shoulders, and Liz Anne finally met her own gaze in the mirror.

Was this a mistake—sinking into his touch, letting herself enjoy it? Bobby had been nothing but kind to her from the beginning. Sweet, talented. And good-looking.

And whatever happened tonight, it didn't have to mean anything more than what it was.

Liz Anne swiped a fresh coat of gloss on her lips and fluffed out her hair. It almost felt normal, primping in front of a mirror while someone waited for her—and not to color or build puzzles.

Messing around with Bobby might not be the responsible choice. But it sure felt good.

Bobby let his fingers fiddle with the strings as he leaned back into the couch. Liz Anne might've hesitated at first, but once she loosened up, she turned soft and sweet. Shy, still. Nervous, maybe, but he could go slow, let his lips work out all that tension. He'd made some pretty good progress with that already.

That sense he'd had that Liz Anne was something special hadn't gone anywhere, but there was so much she was still holding back. If taking his time was the way to go, he sure as hell didn't mind. He had a feeling it'd be worth it. And it wasn't like he didn't have the time.

Footsteps padded down the hall that disappeared past the corner of the living room, and Bobby stopped playing. He grinned up at the figure that halted just in view. Only it wasn't Liz Anne.

A young boy stood frozen, his hair mussed from sleep, faded pajamas hanging loose.

Bobby's grin slipped, and he sat up straighter. "Hi, there."

"Who're you?" the boy asked. His bottom lip stuck out but didn't tremble. But it made more sense now, Liz Anne insisting they couldn't meet anywhere else tonight.

"I'm Bobby." The kid didn't react, so he added, "I've been teaching Liz Anne some guitar."

Small shoulders inched up as the boy clenched his arms tighter in front of him.

"Did the music get you up?" Bobby asked like an idiot.

The boy's head swept side to side, his eyes trained on Bobby.

"D'you play guitar, too?" he asked. Maybe he could show the kid a trick or two while they waited for Liz Anne to come out.

Another head shake. Crinkles appeared on the boy's forehead, a sure sign tears were coming next. But what could he do? Most kids liked Bobby fine. But then most kids didn't wake up in the middle of the night to see him sitting on their couch.

Another door clicked open out of sight, and Bobby's shoulders unclenched. Liz Anne could get her brother back to bed, and maybe the two of them would meet sometime when the kid was in a better mood, or off with their mom.

"Parker," Liz Anne said, still out of sight. A moment later her eyes met Bobby's before she crouched down beside her brother, sweeping the hair she'd let down out of the way. "What're you doing up?"

"Woke up, and you weren't there," the boy muttered in that not-quite-awake way kids had.

Liz Anne's gaze flew to Bobby again. He shot her a smile. "Don't worry, just gave me and your brother a chance to get to know each other a bit."

She straightened from the crouch, one hand wrapping around the boy's shoulders, back in her way-too-serious mode. She leveled a blank but defiant look Bobby's way. "Parker's my son."

Bobby blinked, mind blanking. What could he even say?

She turned to the boy—her *son*—all her attention on him like Bobby wasn't even there. "Let's get you back to bed."

Liz Anne ushered Parker into the bedroom and nudged the door shut. Whatever Bobby was thinking now, it would have to wait.

"What happened?" she asked as Parker settled on his bed. She picked up the Curious George doll from where it'd fallen on the floor, drew the blanket up to Parker's chest, then sat on the edge of the bed.

"Had a nightmare," he said, the hurt in his voice obvious. "And you weren't there."

"I was just in the bathroom, baby." She brushed the matted curls back from his face. "And I'm right here now."

Parker's chest rose and fell a few times, his body already slipping toward sleep. But then he asked, "Who's he?"

Her head turned, leaving her staring at the bedroom wall like she could see clear through to the living room. "That's Mister Bobby. He's been helping me out, teaching me to play better on guitar." She looked back down to Parker, easily visible with the nightlight's glow. "You've heard me practicing," she added.

He nodded, his eyes fighting to stay open. "He a nice teacher?"

Liz Anne swallowed a smile at the edge of protectiveness to Parker's voice. "Yes," she said, nodding back seriously.

Parker inhaled, his chest puffing up before a long sigh sagged his body into the bed. "He plays good," he said, eyelids drooping.

"Yep." It was all so simple in Parker's eyes. Was Bobby nice? Yes. Was he a good guitarist? Also yes. The other pieces were the complicated ones.

With her own small sigh, Liz Anne bent down to brush a kiss on Parker's forehead. "Now close those eyes," she said.

And because everything was easy at five years old, he listened, shutting his eyes with a puffed exhale and a sharp turn of his head away from the light.

Fifteen

It didn't take long for Parker to drift back off to sleep, but by the time Liz Anne walked back into the living room, Bobby and his guitar were gone. And a quick look out the window confirmed his car was gone, too.

Easy.

His shocked expression at learning Parker was her son should have told her everything she needed to know. Of course he'd be gone.

She should have known better than to let her guard down in the first place. She *had* known better. But it'd been so long since anyone treated her as nice as Bobby did, helped her out. Believed in her a little, even.

And the feel of his arms around her, his lips on hers…

Nothing more than a memory now, to be pushed aside if not forgotten.

Liz Anne sank down onto the couch, letting her head drop forward into her hands. Shaky breaths streamed through her lips as prickling built in her eyes. How could she have let things get this far? Forgotten how shocked, judgmental, *appalled* people got when they learned about Parker. Seeing nothing more than a mistake, a loss of virtue, instead of the bright, kind boy.

Tears spilled out of her eyes, wetting her fingers.

She hadn't meant to, but somehow she'd fooled herself into thinking it'd be different with Bobby. That he'd give her the benefit of the doubt after holding her, kissing her, making nice... Or at least he'd stick around to talk to her, not just slip out without a word.

Swallowing back more tears, Liz Anne wiped her cheeks dry, then passed her hands over her jeans. Whatever she'd thought didn't matter now.

She picked up her phone, still resting on the edge of the couch where she'd left it. A message from Bobby waited on the screen.

`Emergency sorry. Talk later.`

Right.

The lie propelled her up off the couch. Life always went on.

She pulled her hair back into a ponytail, picked up the plate of brownies and set it near the fridge, then took out a box of plastic wrap. But instead of tearing off a square of plastic, she lifted a brownie and bit into the gooey chocolate.

By the time the front door opened, Liz Anne was sitting at the kitchen table, halfway through her third brownie and a glass of tea. Momma threw one look her way before turning to shut the door and hang up her purse and jacket on their old coat tree.

"How was your night?" Liz Anne asked. Just because hers hadn't gone to plan, didn't mean she didn't hope her momma'd had a good time with her coworkers. She more than deserved it, even if all her old friends still judged her for Liz Anne's choices.

"Fine, not bad." Momma nodded, taking in the guitar still leaning against the couch, the brownie in Liz Anne's hand, then finally stopping on Liz Anne's face. Were her eyes still red? They had to be, or maybe makeup had smudged down her cheeks, because next thing her momma asked was, "What happened?"

That prickling covered her eyes again, and Liz Anne let the remaining brownie in her hand drop to the napkin on the table. Some part of her ached to cry into her momma's arms, but they'd never really been like that. Momma'd had a hard enough time, raising Liz Anne on her own best she could. Which meant long nights at work and a stern hand at home, though it hadn't exactly paid off the way she'd have wanted.

But she was still Liz Anne's momma.

"He just left." The words popped out as Momma opened the fridge to bring out some potato salad. It sounded so stupid, hovering in the air like that. Of course he'd left, since he wasn't there, and the real problem was why. Liz Anne swirled a sip of tea around her mouth before explaining. "Parker woke up. Guess Bobby thought he was my brother at first, but you know I don't lie about that." Not ever. Parker would never have reason to believe she was ashamed of having him, no matter how much people wanted her to be.

"You're mighty upset for him being just your guitar teacher," Momma pointed out, sitting down at the table with a small plate.

Liz Anne shrugged, poking at the brownie. Momma's silence weighed down on her shoulders as the fork scraped against the plate of salad.

"So why'd he leave?" Momma asked eventually.

"Does it matter?" Liz Anne asked, looking up. "Guys'll say anything to get away, the lies letting them feel like they'd still been polite." Like they had ever since she'd started showing. Liz Anne didn't let it get that far anymore. Normally she was the one making excuses that passed for *no*.

Momma set the fork down, leveling Liz Anne with a look that made her feel like she was back in school. "What did this one say?"

For a moment, she wanted to lie, claim he hadn't said anything at all. Was there any real difference between that and his lie?

But she couldn't be mad at him for lying then turn around and do it, too. "There was some emergency," she admitted.

"And you go on and think the worst."

"What am I supposed to think? He meets Parker and runs off." She sounded younger with each word, but… "That's a mighty big coincidence."

"Seems to me," Momma said slowly, around bites of potato, "you're upset he jumped to conclusions. Didn't think highly enough of you to give you the benefit of the doubt when things turned complicated." Her fork pointed at Liz Anne. "And being a young mother *is* complicated."

Her mouth dry, Liz Anne pushed away the remaining brownie her fingers had crumbled up and took another sip of tea.

"But now you're sitting here, doing the same thing," her momma continued. "Judging him, assuming he's lying, not giving him a chance to explain. When maybe he ain't done nothing wrong."

Liz Anne's lips popped open, but there was nothing to say. She should've known better than to think Momma would understand, sympathize maybe. She hadn't thrown Liz Anne out, helped more than Liz Anne had a right to ask for. But the disappointment still hovered, always there.

Silently, Momma took care of her dishes and headed to bed.

She was right about one thing: no one gave a teen mom the benefit of the doubt. Most everyone conveniently forgot someone else had to be involved for there to be a baby at all. And sure, Liz Anne was used to expecting the worst too, now. Folks didn't give her much reason not to, especially when they found out about Parker.

But Bobby'd been nothing but nice 'til then, ignoring every reason she'd given him not to be. *Had* Liz Anne jumped to conclusions? *Talk soon*, he'd written.

Liz Anne slipped her phone out, staring at Bobby's message for a long while before making herself write:

Hope everything's okay.

Three words. Worst case, she was making a fool of herself. But shoot, she'd gotten over worse. With one more breath, Liz Anne hit SEND.

Sixteen

ou sure you're doing okay?" Bobby asked, helping his mom out of the truck. The doctors had sworn she was fine, that it was only a fall, and not even a bad one, all things considered. No concussion, just a little soreness. And sometimes as folks got older they were more prone to falls.

But the hospital staff didn't know his mom, couldn't know how much she'd changed lately. Thank the Lord one of their tenants had heard her drop a pot or something and gone to check.

Her too fragile hand shook lightly in Bobby's as they made it up the walkway to her building. "You heard the doctors," she said, as if he was worrying for nothing.

Then again, she'd been more herself last night than she usually was lately. Had getting out of the house—even to the hospital—helped her shake loose some of that recent confusion?

She swatted his hand away when he started to unlock the door, taking the keys herself.

"You worried me, that's all," Bobby said, following her into the apartment. A pot, a knife, and some onions lay scattered on the kitchen floor. Ignoring them, Bobby placed an arm around her shoulders and led her to her favorite chair in the living room.

"Nothing to worry about," she insisted, getting herself settled. "I fell. It happens." Her arm gently tugged him down until he sat on the end of the couch nearest her. "You tell me about you instead."

"Ain't much to tell. Memorial Day's coming up, and Kane's invited us for that big barbecue again." Hell, he was supposed to head back out with Kane tomorrow, not back until late Sunday night, just in time for the celebration. But Bobby couldn't leave his mom alone after a fall. There were nurses or some such he could hire, right? To check in while he was out of the city. Maybe he'd ask Mrs. Cotten for the next few days. Then maybe he'd move back in.

His mom nodded, the distant look of long-lost memories creeping over her eyes, like now that she was home, she could slip back into the past.

Bobby leaned forward, taking her hand again. "You want me to play a little something for you?"

She blinked, then startled, like she hadn't expected to see him there. "No." Bobby frowned, but she squeezed his hand and added, "I want us to talk."

Dread pitted in his stomach, but Bobby nodded. "Okay. You want me to make you some hot tea?" She'd lived in Tennessee most of her life, but she'd never gotten used to the sweet iced version everyone here drank.

"All right." She smiled, letting go of him and allowing her weight to relax into the chair. "But then you tell me what you've been doing with yourself lately."

Bobby stooped to pick up the things she'd dropped in her fall, then set the kettle on the stove. "Pretty much the usual, Ma. Playing with Kane, backing some folks in the studio."

The back of her head bobbed in acknowledgment. "You been seeing anyone?"

Bobby froze. It wasn't the sort of thing they talked about, most times. "I ain't been lonely, if that's what you mean."

She scoffed, and Bobby's frown deepened, before slipping into a rueful smile. At least she was showing some spirit, even if the question was uncomfortable. Did he even know the answer at this point?

He hadn't stopped laying on the charm with girls he met at their gigs, but he also hadn't slept with any of them in a while. Not that he'd been angling to get Liz Anne into bed, either. And now that it turned out she had a kid…

No wonder she was wound so tight all the time.

Shaking his head, Bobby poured the tea, then brought it out to his mom and set it on the side table beside her.

She twisted the handle toward her but didn't lift the cup, letting it cool. "So?" she asked as he took his spot on the couch. "It's past time for you to find someone good, Robi."

"I don't know, Mom." Bobby leaned his elbows on his knees, pressing his knuckles into the palm of the other hand. "I've been spending some time with someone, but…"

Her eyes sharpened on him. "But?"

"It's complicated."

"Not everything can be easy." Sadness slid into her expression, drawing her away again.

"I know," Bobby said quickly. "And I'd love your advice." He wanted to keep her there with him, sure, but maybe she'd help him get his head on straight, too.

She refocused on him a moment, a few seconds passing before she really seemed to recognize him. Then she shook her head and reached for the tea.

"Not much has happened," Bobby said. "She's this new singer, all business. But I thought there might be something there."

His mom hummed as she sipped, confirming she was listening.

"But she has a kid."

His mom's eyebrows drew together, the concern in her eyes clear.

So he wasn't crazy. This was definitely a game changer. Bobby leaned back, scrubbing his palms on his jeans. "I just found out," he continued, "don't know what the story is. But—" Liz Anne wouldn't have kissed him like that if the boy's father was still around, right? He sighed again. Did it matter? "Guess I didn't realize how much I thought there was a chance, that this'd go somewhere. But with a kid? It ain't like I can ignore him while his mom and I figure out if we even like each other enough to give it a go."

He swallowed past the lump clogging his throat. "And who am I to be someone's—" He bit down before saying the word *father*. Maybe a decade from now, but it was way too soon for him to take on that kind of responsibility. He liked kids, sure, palled around with ones he met. But that wasn't the same thing as *raising* one.

By the time he brought himself to look back at his mom, her face was pinched in a frown that shouted her disappointment. "Did this girl ask you to be her son's father?"

Sticky sweat coated the back of his neck. Bobby swept it away with one hand. "No."

"No," she repeated. The teacup *thunked* against the table, underscoring the syllable. "So you're here inventing problems. Now"—she held a hand up to stop his protest—"if you don't like this girl, that's okay. Maybe she's not right for you. And no one's asking you to jump head first into their family. But you see a little challenge, questions about the future, and you're running the other way." Her head shook, the frown lines deepening. "Like always."

The breath whooshed out of him, straightening Bobby up out of his seat. "What's that mean?" He stalked across the room then spun back around to face her. "I've built a pretty good career so far, Ma."

She took a long draw of tea, like she hadn't just tipped his world a little further off-kilter. "So far," she echoed after lowering the cup. "But you always said you were going to do more,

more than playing in bars, out all hours of the night. Like teaching."

His heart settled, the anxiety of the last twelve hours, sparked on by this conversation, deflating. "I still might, someday." There was plenty of time for all that when he wouldn't have enough work from playing. And what did this have to do with Liz Anne and her kid?

Bobby's mom held out her hand, and he crossed to her side to take it, crouching by the chair. "You've been blessed," she said, "with a beautiful gift. It's the one thing you've truly worked for. But it's also come easier for you than most people. Your talent built your life, gave you your spot with Kane, and Lord knows I'm proud every time I hear you play." Her fingers tightened in his. "Your dad, too."

She paused, and Bobby bent his head to avoid the tears glittering in her eyes.

"But you never had to fight for it, Robi. And you never much liked thinking of the future, nothing past next week or next month. Not with school, and hardly even with the guitar."

Her hand slipped down to her lap, and Bobby shifted back up onto the couch. He'd made his plan, and then he'd made it happen. Getting that spot with Kane had opened doors, sure. And he'd put himself out there to get it, worked to keep it.

But it was true that since then he'd had steady work, and if one thing fell through, another would come up soon enough.

He didn't exactly need a long-term plan. Being good on guitar was about all he had to offer the world, so that was what he did.

And once his dad passed, he'd focused on keeping the building running, being there for his mom. Not that that was especially hard, but it filled the days he wasn't working.

"When the future comes up," his mom went on, "you see the hard work it could take, every way things could go wrong. And you figure it's not worth trying. But if you don't try, things won't ever have a chance to go right."

She exhaled roughly, twice, the sounds piercing through him. He shouldn't have let her get so worked up.

Bobby cupped his hand on her shoulder, careful not to press too hard. "It's okay, Mom."

"I want more for you than just paying the rent," she said, holding his gaze straight on.

"I do, too," he assured. Didn't he? The future had a way of working itself out, and meanwhile he had the music.

But everything was different with a kid in the picture. Was he getting ahead of things? Hell, Liz Anne hadn't even meant for him to meet her son. Wasn't like she was trying to rope him into anything.

Bobby shook the questions away and shot his mom a smile. "How's about I go pick us up some lunch?"

Seventeen

"G̶o get dressed," Liz Anne said Memorial Day morning, shooing Parker to the bedroom. When he'd called to confirm the invitation, Dennings said the whole thing was pretty casual, but her heart was still hammering, and they needed to get going if they wanted to make it out to Nashville at a reasonable time.

If she hadn't promised Parker he could come watch her play, she would've backed out.

It didn't help that all she'd heard from Bobby was a quick, "See you Monday." Did he want to ignore what they'd done? Get back to teacher–student—or maybe not even that? She'd go with whatever he chose. Better than making a scene in front of Kane, and his manager, and all their friends…

She'd lost her mind, agreeing to this. So excited for another chance to play—who knew what sort of folks Kane had invited?—she hadn't thought it through. There might be some important people listening, sure. But they might hear her fail.

Sighing, Liz Anne pulled the giant bowl of Momma's macaroni salad out of the fridge, then patted her pockets to check for her phone and keys.

Parker came running out, proudly displaying the shorts and tee she'd laid out on the bed that he'd put on, right side out and everything.

"Sunscreen," she reminded. "And shoes!" she called after him as he disappeared. He'd already had a pretty great weekend, what with her momma taking him to the splash zone opening over in Franklin on Saturday, and their day out at Bowie Park yesterday. It hadn't been much in the way of a hike, but Parker had loved it. And Liz Anne's feet sure didn't mind keeping their nature walk short. Only problem was, she'd forgotten the sunscreen, leaving them both a bit too pink. Not a mistake she wanted to make twice.

Liz Anne checked the salad, her purse, and the waiting guitar again, then made her way to the other bedroom. Quietly rapping on the door, she asked, "Are you about ready, Momma?"

Parker tugged on her hand before she heard an answer. A chuckle bubbled up out of her throat at the white streaks covering his face and arms.

"C'mere," she said, brushing her hands over his face to swipe off the extra sunscreen. She scrubbed the lotion on her own face, then did the same with his arms. Maybe there'd be some kids at this thing. Then it almost wouldn't matter if Liz Anne made a fool of herself playing, so long as Parker had a normal day of fun.

Momma joined them as Parker scrambled into the car, then stretched out his arms for the bowl of salad. Liz Anne tucked her guitar in the back seat, rounded the car, and slipped in behind the wheel. Momma climbed in silently, but that was better than her comments on the "sort" of people they'd be seeing. Meaning musicians, which might as well have been a dirty word, the way her momma felt. Hopefully this barbecue would surprise her, help her see a good life could be built on playing for folks.

"Seatbelt?" Liz Anne reminded over her shoulder, twisting the key in the ignition.

The engine sputtered, choking a bit, then revved up and—

Died.

Momma's sigh echoed in the silence where the engine's rumble should have been.

"What's wrong?" Parker asked, still eager to get going.

"I don't know, baby." *Lord, please*, Liz Anne prayed, twisting the key again.

Nothing.

"Okay," Liz Anne said, mostly to herself. She bent down to pop the hood, not that she had any real idea what she'd be looking at.

"Let's get that salad back in the house," Momma said, getting out of the car and opening Parker's door.

"No," he said, whipping Liz Anne's head around to him. "You said we could go." His bottom lip stuck out in stubborn pout.

"The car won't—" Liz Anne began to say.

"You promised!"

She met Momma's eyes over Parker's head. He hardly ever acted out, even when he maybe had a right to.

"You promised I'd hear you play," he said, sullen, little arms wrapped around the bowl dwarfing him in the seat.

Liz Anne slumped in her seat. "I can still play for you, just for you."

Parker's jaw shifted in his pout, but he didn't meet her gaze, staring at the seatback in front of him. Her momma went over to the front of the car, lifting the hood. She helped out with Parker, but she'd long ago made clear that he was Liz Anne's responsibility, first and foremost.

With a deep breath, Liz Anne twisted further in the seat so she could reach Parker's arm. "Baby, the car is broken. I know you're disappointed, but we don't exactly got a spare."

Finally he looked at her, his eyes scrunched up but not with tears. He was thinking up something, and this wasn't exactly the best of timing. Liz Anne still had to call Dennings and explain. How unprofessional would *that* look? There went any chance of being asked to play with Kane again, that was for sure.

Liz Anne shut her eyes against the building frustration. Just another day with no good choices. And a holiday, to boot, so she had to find a way to make it up to Parker. If she ever got him out of the car.

"Your friend," he said quietly, snapping her eyes open.

"What?" Liz Anne asked. She didn't exactly have loads of friends ready to do her big favors. Or any friends, really.

"Your guitar friend," Parker repeated. His eyes weren't scrunched up any more, and the pout was gone. But this might've been worse. *Bobby*? "He's been here."

"Yeah. Yep, he has."

"He got a car."

Liz Anne's jaw popped open as her brain froze. "Yep, he does." Asking Bobby to drive all the way out here and come get them all—then drive them back? Insane, in adult world. But in kid world…

"And friends do nice things for friends." Parker paused, face scrunching up again like he wasn't sure of what he'd said. Guilt stabbed through Liz Anne at his uncertainty. "Right?"

The house door slapped closed as Momma made her way back inside, probably tired of waiting for this standoff to end.

It wasn't like Liz Anne could let Parker sit all day in the car, even if calling Bobby might be worse than never being able to face Dennings or Kane again. But shoot, if this was what it took to make Parker happy, even for an afternoon, then she could stomach it. "Tell you what. You get out of this car, get that salad back in the fridge,"—she sighed—"and I'll call Mister Bobby and ask."

Lord only knew how she'd repay him if he said yes.

✧ ✧ ✧

Bobby grit his teeth and tapped the steering wheel as he pulled up to Liz Anne's house. She'd practically choked on the words, asking him if he might—if it wasn't too much trouble, and of course she'd pay him back for the gas soon as she could—come by and give them a ride out to Kane's. If Kane's wife, Sabella, hadn't been around to keep an eye on his mom, he might've said no. Or sent Steve.

But his mom was safe with Sabella, and hell, it was just a ride. An hour out of his day.

A little head popped up over the porch the minute Bobby hit the brakes. No smile, but there was no hiding the kid was excited. Was Liz Anne?

Bobby was somewhere in the middle, about seeing her again. It could go so many ways, most of them awkward or downright bad.

But that didn't change everything he'd seen in her before. Or how good she felt in his arms, how fun it was, breaking through all those walls.

Built to protect her son, no doubt.

Didn't mean she had to give up on her own life, though, right? Question was whether Bobby wanted to be a part of it. If she'd even let him.

All questions that didn't need to matter today.

Bobby got out of the car and lifted a hand in greeting as Liz Anne came out of the house holding a big bowl. She said something that he couldn't make out and her son probably ignored, running toward Bobby's car with her guitar case held out in front of him. He stopped a few feet short, eyes wide, head tilted. Seeing if Bobby measured up.

Bobby shot him an easy grin. "Parker, right? Dunno if you remember, but I'm Bobby."

"I 'member," Parker said in that far too serious way some kids had.

Liz Anne caught up to them, shifting the bowl to one hip so she could lay a hand on Parker's shoulder. Her type of serious was different, back to her closed-off shell. "Thank you for this." She looked down to her kid, mouth slipping into a small smile. "We're all real excited."

She half-turned away and gestured behind her. "This here's my momma, Corinne. Momma, this is Bobby." She hesitated a moment, then added, "My guitar teacher."

Bobby ramped up the charm again, nodding to the older woman in a gray-and-blue dress that looked more suited for an office than a backyard barbecue. "Ma'am."

She dipped her chin in return. "Kind of you to do this."

"Oh, well, couldn't let y'all miss out on the fun. What do you say?" he asked, focusing on the boy who fidgeted where he stood, waiting for some kind of permission to climb in the car. "We ready to go?"

Eighteen

iz Anne glanced over at Bobby for the millionth time, then back out at the road. Silence stuffed every corner of the car now that Parker had run out of questions to ask Bobby. Or maybe he'd gotten nervous, knowing there'd be other kids there. He hadn't asked his usual, "Think they'll like me?" But Lord, she hoped so. His classmates would've, too, if their folks hadn't gotten in the way with all their sanctimonious nonsense. Now each time Parker had a chance to meet someone new, he worried.

But the folks at the barbecue wouldn't know she'd never been married. Question was, would anyone be looking at her and doing the math?

Liz Anne turned to check on Parker in the back seat, buckled in behind Bobby. But Parker was staring out the window now, too. As she twisted back around, Bobby caught her eye, looking at her a moment too long before getting his eyes back on the road.

What was he thinking? She never should've asked him for

the ride. But Parker had been so upset… And besides, he'd said yes. To be polite?

Liz Anne scrubbed the sweat coating her palms off onto her jeans. She'd paired them with one of her nicer tops, a delicate, pale-green one that draped softly and felt more festive than a tee shirt. First impressions and all.

They had to be pretty close now, driving past rows of houses. No peeling paint or dying lawns in this neighborhood. Liz Anne blew her breath out, counting to ten. Parker'd pick up on her nerves in a second if she didn't calm down.

Sure enough, when they'd all piled out of the car in front of a brick one-story house, Parker pressed into her side. Good-natured noise floated to them from around back, laughter and talking and all the signs of folks having a good time.

Bobby's eyes raked over the three of them, and Liz Anne set her free hand on Parker's shoulder. She couldn't even begin to guess what her momma was thinking. When was the last time any of them had gone to a neighborhood barbecue?

"Them folks won't bite," Bobby said, and Parker shuffled a little closer to her. Bobby tried to smile, but mostly looked like he thought they'd lost their minds. That wasn't what mattered right now.

"You ready, baby?" Liz Anne asked Parker.

He shrugged against her side, digging his toes into the dirt.

"Come all this way, we can't just stand around on the street here," her momma said, trying to help in her own way.

Liz Anne took a deep breath, then filled all her fake waitress cheer into her voice. "This is going to be so much fun, I betcha I'll be dragging you away by the end of the day."

"Y'know, I'll tell y'all a secret," Bobby said, tucking his thumbs into his pockets. "I could take or leave the folks themselves, but the *food* Mr. and Mrs. Hartridge have got there, well. Wouldn't want to pass that up."

"Good to know," a new voice said, snapping Liz Anne's focus to a woman standing a few feet away on the walk, shaking her head at Bobby, who grinned back. The woman, maybe a few years older than Liz Anne, turned her smile on the three of them. "Welcome," she said. "You must be Liz Anne. And…"

"My son, Parker," Liz Anne introduced. "And my momma, Corinne Layton."

"So glad you could join us," the woman said, sounding like she meant it, even.

"This here's Sabella, Kane's wife," Bobby explained. Sabella's mouth twitched into a small smile at the word *wife*.

"Thank you for having us, Mrs. Hartridge," Liz Anne said.

"Oh, call me Sabella, please," Kane's wife answered with another easy smile. "For all of Bobby's faults, he was right about one thing. We have loads of food waiting in the backyard, though that pasta salad looks amazing. It was so nice of you to bring that."

"Our pleasure," Momma said, probably still trying to figure out what to make of Kane's wife. Like all of them were.

"What do you say, Parker?" Sabella asked. "Do you want to come check out what else we have?"

Parker hesitated, then looked up at Liz Anne. For a moment, she wanted to hug him close instead of letting him go off with this overly nice stranger. But that wasn't why they'd come, and Liz Anne'd be right behind them anyway. "Go on," she said, giving him a little nudge.

"Did you help make all that salad?" Sabella asked as Parker stepped toward her.

"Yes, ma'am."

"I'm so impressed. Kane likes to cook, but I've never seen him make something like pasta salad before."

Bobby chuckled, shaking his head, but Parker seemed to be warming up to Sabella, following her around the house to the back.

"She's very welcoming," Liz Anne said.

"She's a good one," Bobby agreed, holding her gaze an extra moment again. Then he gestured the way Sabella had gone. "Shall we, ladies?"

Both the Layton women looked like they were about to stroll into a nest of vipers, not enjoy some good barbecue in better company. Seemed Mrs. Layton was strung even tighter than her daughter.

When the three of them passed through the open gate into the Hartridges' backyard, the women stalled, taking in the scene like they were planning out a battle strategy.

Bobby's mom sat over in the shade by a little glass table, the matching seat filled by a woman he'd never met. But they seemed to be enjoying their chat, eyes on the center of the yard where Sabella stood with a group of kids, no doubt introducing Parker to the others.

Kane was over by the grill with Mr. Burnett, having a beer and arguing over sauces or marinades or the perfect temperature for a grill. Mrs. Burnett, meanwhile, was over by the food table with some of the other women, making sure everything was in easy reach and no empty dish stayed out for long. Others drifted up to fill their plates, exchanging smiles and greetings, and compliments on this year's food.

Bobby steered Liz Anne and her mom over so they could find a spot for their salad, meet some folks, and maybe even start to relax. He made the introductions then offered to grab some drinks. Both Liz Anne and her mom declined. No surprise there. Still he stepped away to grab himself a beer. Maybe they'd be more comfortable with the other women if he wasn't at their side.

He grabbed a bottle from the ice chest with a quick hello to Cash Grady, another singer Bobby sometimes backed, and his very pregnant wife.

While Bobby'd been gone, the raised wood platform on the far side of the yard had been set up with Steve's drums and stands for people's guitars. At some point, someone would kick things off, be the first to play a couple songs. Then Kane'd invite some of the others up to take a spin. Including Liz Anne, at some point.

And finally the three of them would wrap things up with some of Kane's favorites, or songs their friends called out, if he was in the mood. It was going to be a good day.

Parker caught sight of his mom and broke away from the other kids, coming to a halt at her side. Liz Anne instantly crouched down beside him, running her eyes over him, head to toe, like it hadn't been only a couple minutes since he'd left her side.

The kid looked at the spread of food before him, expression growing serious again. Then he asked for some macaroni salad. Like he wasn't allowed to want anything else. Bobby almost walked over to pile the kid a heaping plate of everything on the table.

But Mrs. Burnett overheard, and soon she was tugging Parker and Liz Anne along, explaining what all kinds of food they had, and which drinks were only for adults. A couple of the other kids plucked plates off the table, the nearby adults helping to fill them up. Soon most of the kids were sitting in the grass, faces smeared with bits of everything on their plates. Parker hesitated, but then Grady's daughter asked him something or other, and he started gobbling things up with the rest of them. And the women occupied themselves with Liz Anne and Mrs. Layton, asking them all sorts of chatty questions.

Bobby shook his head at his own nonsense, getting nearly as stressed as Liz Anne was. These were good people, and she'd be fine without him.

So long as his mom was feeling okay and having a good time, he had nothing to worry about. Exactly how he liked it.

Nineteen

Everyone at the Hartridges' was being so nice that Liz Anne's head was spinning. Momma might not have made friends, exactly, but she'd been invited to a ladies' quilting night. Maybe if she went, friendship with some of these women wasn't too far behind. Course, first they had to get the car fixed.

But Parker was having an amazing time, running around with the other kids. So this whole thing was already worth it. Earlier the kids had tossed a football around with some of the men. One of them had even taken the time to show Parker how to hold it right.

When Liz Anne had gone to thank him, he'd shot her a big smile. "Great kid you got there," he'd said, before asking how Liz Anne knew the Hartridges.

"I opened for Kane a couple times," she admitted. "Awfully kind of him to include us today."

"So you're playing later, then?" asked a woman who overheard, reaching past Liz Anne to grab a lingering pastry ball loaded up with cheese.

"Only reason she came," said a familiar voice. Bobby grinned at their little group, and the others laughed, saying they looked forward to it.

"Doing all right?" he asked when the others stepped away. He filled a small plate with grapes and strawberries, and a square of hummingbird cake that looked as impressive as the rest of the food had been. Hard to believe it was all homemade. But Momma's macaroni salad had held its own, the bowl almost emptied before it had been moved into the house with the other dishes to make way for desserts.

Bobby glanced up from the table, eyebrows rounding.

He'd asked her something… "Of course," she said, a moment too late.

His eyes narrowed, but he just nodded once, then reached for a second small plate. He plopped another piece of cake on it, grabbed a fork, and put it in Liz Anne's hands.

By the time her brain caught up, he was back at the side of an older woman he'd been looking after all day. She smiled up at him as he set the other plate by her elbow, then he settled in the grass by her feet to listen to the duo up on the small stage.

Once the music had started, most everyone's chatter had quieted down. Except the kids, who were running around squirting each other with small water pistols. One of them had even handed an orange one to Parker, who had the biggest smile she'd ever seen. Warmth squeezed around Liz Anne's heart and spread through her chest as tears prickled at her eyes.

None of the parents had pulled their kids away from playing with her son. No one seemed to be whispering about the frayed hem of his jeans, or how sad it was, growing up with a mother like her. Might've been different if they knew, but they didn't, and Lord was it a breath of fresh air. Even more reason to get out of Fairview, just as soon as they could.

Liz Anne glanced at the plate in her hands, with thick layers of cake covered in creamy white icing and a sprinkling of pecans. Letting it go to waste would be a shame. So she found an empty chair, smiled at the folks sitting nearby, and dug her fork in.

"So what's the verdict?" Sabella asked as Bobby popped open a fresh beer.

He offered it to her, but she shook her head and peered into the ice bucket. He shrugged and took a sip. She shifted some of the bottles around, then pulled out a lemonade.

"Well?" she added, twisting off the top.

"Not bad." He grinned. "Course I know Kane did all the work."

"Damn straight," she said in her best attempt at a drawl.

"Now you come in here, taking all the credit." He elbowed her arm gently, though by now she definitely knew he was kidding.

"The secret to married life," she teased back.

Truth was, back when it'd been just Kane, everything had been a bit more…rugged. Basic. Fancy equipment was saved for the platform stage. Everything else was about big portions, burgers tossed on the grill, and enough beers to go around. When the neighbors started joining and it turned into a potluck, plastic tablecloths had appeared, along with serving utensils, and things like juices and pie, plus some folding chairs for those who didn't like the grass. With Sabella around, everything looked a bit smoother—nice gingham tablecloths, pitchers of sangria, platters laid out in fancy patterns of fruit or, earlier on, fixings for the burgers, even themed napkins instead of rolls of paper towels. And Kane had showed off some of his fancy cooking skills. Different, but not in a bad way.

Across the yard, Cash kicked into an upbeat little two-step, fumbled the words, laughed, and started over again. That was the great thing about these barbecues—everything was casual, friendly. No pressure.

Even Liz Anne looked like she'd relaxed, smiling at the kids and soaking in everyone's carefree chatter.

"You really like her," Sabella said beside him.

Bobby lifted the forgotten beer to his lips and angled his body away from the *her* in question, like he simply wanted to move closer to Sabella. "Who?"

Sabella frowned like a disappointed parent. She'd make a good mom, whenever she and Kane had kids. "Don't play dumb."

Bobby took a deep breath and dropped the smile. A concerned crinkle appeared between Sabella's eyebrows. "Maybe," Bobby told her. "But it's all too complicated."

"How so?"

"Well let's start with her son, sitting right over there in the middle of your yard."

One of Kane's neighbors strolled up to grab a fresh drink, and Bobby and Sabella both smiled at him. She set her hand on Bobby's arm and shifted them a few steps away from all the food. She glanced over at the group of kids, raptly listening to the music, then her gaze met Bobby's. "Something tells me of everyone here you'll have the fewest problems finding common ground with a five-year-old," Sabella said with a small smile that was closer to a smirk.

He couldn't exactly argue with that. But playing around with the kid wasn't the problem.

"Look," Sabella said, all trace of humor replaced with her direct earnestness. "Don't you think it's time you stopped fooling around with whatever girl smiles your way while you're on stage? What am I saying,"—she held up a hand to ward off his answer—"of course you do. You already have."

Bobby's jaw shifted, and he clamped it shut. He would've figured the guys had better things to think about than who he was sleeping with. Even if he *hadn't* been with anyone when they'd been out on tour this time. But if no girl had caught his eye, that was his business.

"All I'm saying," Sabella continued, "is that it might be time for you to take a chance on something real, something more significant than a few hours of fun. Maybe it won't work out. But maybe…" Her attention strayed to Kane, who was calling up the next singer. Her face softened into an easy contentment. "Maybe it'll be extraordinary."

Bobby choked a sip of beer past the lump in his throat.

Fist clenched around the neck of her guitar, Liz Anne took the spot in front of the mic and thanked Kane. Her nerves were back, if not quite in full swing. She settled on the barstool someone had brought out from the kitchen a while back. The colors of the sunset cascaded through the length of her hair as she swept it back from her face. Bobby shook the thought away.

"Such a pleasure meeting all y'all today," Liz Anne was saying with her not-quite-real smile. "This song I'd like to sing for you…" Her eyes found her son, who'd moved to sit closer to his grandma, and all the tension seemed to leave with her next exhale. "This is one I wrote about the most important person in my life."

After nodding a few silent counts, like Bobby'd told her to do instead of fiddling with the guitar strings, she began the song they'd most worked on. Before the first verse started, her fingers picked out the melody he'd taught her, not even stumbling this time around. So she'd found time to practice while he'd been gone.

When the sun sinks down low, and I've lost my spark…

Bobby'd heard her sing this one plenty of times by now. But not like this.

Not with the simple honesty of singing to her son.

My arms ache to hold you, keep you safe through the night…

Bobby cleared his throat and started to take a swig of his beer.

But Sabella was staring at him with a pleased but curious expression he couldn't quite figure out. "Extraordinary," she repeated quietly, before being waved over by Cash's wife.

Bobby caught himself shaking his head again and downed the rest of his beer instead, making sure not to crumple the empty can in his fingers while Liz Anne sang.

Her gaze locked on to Bobby's as she sang her last line. "And whispered pleas fall from my lips." Those lips curved up a little, a line of tension building between her and Bobby until she exhaled and glanced around at everyone listening.

"Forgetting something?" Steve asked, jolting Bobby out of his thoughts. He held out Bobby's bass, drumsticks waiting in his other hand.

Oh, right. They were supposedly to play soon. "Thanks." Bobby worked up a smile and crushed the can he still held, taking the instrument. After all, playing was what he was here for.

Twenty

*L*iz Anne met Bobby's eyes in the rearview mirror as he shut off the engine back in front of their house. Silence replaced the music Bobby'd switched on for the ride, punctuated by Parker's soft, sleepy sighs.

As the others got out, Liz Anne gently shook Parker awake.

"Any time, Mrs. Layton," Bobby was saying as Liz Anne nudged her son out of the car. "I'm glad y'all had a good time."

Liz Anne passed the empty bowl out to her momma, then bent down to Parker. "Go on inside and get washed up for bed. I'll be in in a minute."

"Thanks, Mister Bobby," Parker muttered, half asleep, and followed Momma up the walk.

Liz Anne reached into the truck for her guitar, palmed the door closed, and took a deep breath before turning to face Bobby. "You must be sick of hearing us thank you," she tried to joke. The light from their porch fought the night's darkness but not enough for her to read his expression.

"Guess we should talk," he said.

The fake cheer dropped off her face as she nodded. "I have to get Parker to bed," she pointed out quietly. The weight of everything unsaid pressed in around her. In her life, Parker came first. Always.

"I'll wait," Bobby said.

They both stalled until Liz Anne broke through the phantom pressure holding her in place. Bobby followed her silently up to the porch.

"Get you something?" she asked automatically, opening the door.

"I'm fine, thanks." He took a couple steps away, toward the railing.

All she could say was, "Okay." She left the door propped open, but Bobby was obviously too uncomfortable to come into the house now that he knew. Would he even still be out there when she got Parker to sleep?

Bobby leaned his elbows on the railing, staring out at the quiet of Liz Anne's street. A few of the houses had a light on here or there. A dog let out three staccato barks, answered by guttural croaks of a frog or two and what even sounded like the hoots of an owl. Bobby's phone chirped, and he pulled it out to check that the Burnetts had gotten his mom home all right. She'd had fun tonight, been just about her old self with everyone. He'd really need to find a way to get her out of the house more, it seemed. Easier said than done, with them heading to tour the

West Coast soon. Even after he moved back in, he'd have to figure something out for all the times he wasn't going to be home.

Behind him, the door creaked open, and Liz Anne walked out with two glasses of tea. She looked older, somehow, with her hair pulled into a messy ponytail thing and a dark sweater swallowing her torso. As the door swung shut, she reached out a glass for him.

"Thank you," Bobby said and took a sip, more because that was the right thing to do than because he actually wanted it. But the tea wasn't bad, with a hint of peaches.

Liz Anne's lips quirked up for a moment. Then she stepped over to the simple wooden bench nestled against the house. She curled into one corner, tucking one leg under herself as she hugged the other knee close. Sadness or maybe resignation clung to her as she watched him. Bobby leaned back against the porch rail.

Her shoulders dropped, and she set her own glass beside her on the bench. "You must have questions."

That was one way of putting it. Bobby could've figured it out, maybe, if he'd known her better. How young had she been when she'd had her son? Had she married young, out of high school? It wasn't all that rare. Where was the kid's father? "Wouldn't know where to start," he said.

Liz Anne nodded, her gaze drifting to the space between them. "Well." Her chin came up, eyes meeting his as her shoulders pulled back into that ramrod-straight posture. "I was eighteen, when I had Parker. Lucky me, he was a summer baby, so I managed to finish high school first."

Bobby exhaled, his weight sagging into the railing propping him up. Pregnant in high school wasn't exactly rare, either. Hell, Bobby'd had a couple near misses himself. And it seemed she'd managed well enough. "Couldn't have been easy."

She scoffed with a small shake of her head, looking out at the darkness beyond the glow of the porch light. The small movement seemed to slice through the barrier dividing their spots on the porch, letting Bobby move to the other end of her bench.

He sat in silence for a bit before asking, "What about his dad?"

Liz Anne's head swiveled around to him. "Not around." Her fingers tapped against her thigh a couple times. "He, uh. Well." She sighed, then lifted the tea to her lips before setting it back down without even a sip. "You really want to know?"

Shadows deepened the lines of Bobby's frown. Any minute now, he'd get up and walk out into the night. She'd always be grateful for Bobby's help, for the lessons, and most of all for the great day he'd given Parker. But Lord knew there were plenty of girls out there who could offer him more without all the pressure, the complications of having a kid involved.

"It's all right," Liz Anne started to say as he said, "Yeah."

He shot her a look, eyebrows drawing down over his eyes. "Yeah," he repeated, "I want to know."

Twenty-One

*L*iz Anne took a deep breath, filling her lungs to bursting, then slowly blew it out. Everyone in Fairview knew what happened, or thought they did, rumors filling in the gaps in people's memories. Or just complicating things to help the story along. Had she ever actually told anyone what happened? Except telling her momma she was pregnant once she'd started to show, she'd kept it all to herself. And no one had really asked.

Liz Anne wrapped her arms around herself, then dropped them down. "Senior year, there was this party." She forced her gaze back to Bobby's face. His expression didn't change, but he leaned back into the bench, just watching her. "One of the local boys was home from Basic Training, he'd brought some friends back with him." She'd jumped in a friend's car without a second thought, and they'd driven out to an old barn, filled that night with as much booze as hay.

"One of them, he was nice, funny," she continued. "Older, a little." And in great shape from boot camp. "There weren't too many of us there, and somehow we kept finding our way back to each other. He'd bring me fresh drinks, or, I think, maybe we even danced a bit at some point." She shook her head, gripping the glass in front of her to stay in the present.

Bobby's hand landed on her knee.

"No, it wasn't…" Liz Anne licked her lips, then tried again. She didn't want to give him the wrong idea. "We were just having fun. By the end of the night, we were both pretty drunk." She shrugged. "It just happened." In the dark, around back behind the barn. He'd even been a pretty good kisser, from what she remembered. She gulped some tea to wipe away the thought.

Bobby's hand didn't move. He just waited for her to go on.

"When I found out I was pregnant, I tracked him down." He'd thought she was some lovesick teenager, pining for him. "I told him, and he said he'd send me some money." She swallowed past the nothing filling her throat. "To 'take care of it.'"

Bobby's jaw shifted, but he still didn't say anything.

"I thought about it, you know," she admitted. Not that she'd even know where to go.

"Makes sense," Bobby said, pulling his hand back. He shifted, turning more toward her. His hand landed on the back of the bench. "Thinking about all your options, I mean."

"He sent me the money, just like he'd said. But I couldn't do it. Too many Sundays spent in church, maybe." Liz Anne puffed her breath out between her lips, stretching the stiffness out of them. Every bit of her felt stuck, frozen on the bench, so she dragged her body up and crossed the porch.

"Never heard from him again," she added, shaking off the past. She turned back around to the man who *was* here, now. *For now.* "And you're right, it wasn't easy. And the people 'round here... Bet you can imagine." At least Walt had let her keep her job at the diner, even if that brought on rumors the baby had been his. "But Parker's worth it—worth everything to me."

What was there to say to that? It made sense now, all that battle-ready tension Bobby'd had to fight through to get to know her. And of course Liz Anne loved her kid. Hell, Bobby liked the little guy well enough. "He's a good kid."

Liz Anne smiled, almost like she couldn't help it. "Yeah."

Bobby stood and joined her by the railing. Her face tilted up to look at him. They were close enough to kiss, if it wasn't for the invisible fortress surrounding her. "So what now?" he asked quietly.

Her eyes dipped to his lips, and her own popped gently open. Then she turned away with a sharp sigh. "Parker, he's old enough to understand his daddy ain't around. I tell him he's off protecting us all, but..." She shook her head again, staring at the house like she could see clear through to her son's bed. Her hands gripped the railing behind her. "Not even sure he's still alive."

Bobby leaned his elbows beside his abandoned glass of tea.

"I don't date, or whatever," she said quietly, then turned toward him, letting go of the porch. "I can't bring someone into

Parker's life who might up and disappear when things don't work out."

"And I wouldn't want to be that guy."

Liz Anne wrapped her arms around herself. Her head tilted sadly as she shrugged. "Then there ain't anything more to talk about, is there?"

Bobby nodded, letting his head drop. Sure, there might be something between them, but they barely even knew what that was. Maybe it'd be "extraordinary," like Sabella said, but more than likely, it'd end up a mess. And Liz Anne was right—there was too much at stake with a kid involved.

He straightened, gazing out into the street as the crotchety frogs filled the silence. So much could go wrong if they decided to give this thing a shot.

But Bobby's mom was right, too: nothing could go right, if they didn't give it a chance to.

A small chuckle worked itself out of his mouth.

Liz Anne's eyes narrowed, and she took a step back.

"You're doing the same thing I do, or some folks say I do," he explained so she wouldn't take offense. "Seeing how everything could go bad. But what we're both ignoring…" He closed the distance between them. "Is how it could go good."

Her hands slid down her arms, letting go of the protective grip. She tucked them into her back pockets. "What're you saying?"

"I'm saying, we oughtta give this a shot before deciding it'll ruin your life. Or your son's." He set his hands on her waist, which pinned the sweater to her so it clung to her torso as she inhaled roughly. "Haven't ruined it so far, have I?"

Twenty-Two

*L*ord, what was wrong with her? Standing there, thinking about it, just because he hadn't run the other way.

Bobby's smile slipped into something darker, hotter, and Liz Anne's hands moved to rest above his elbows.

His throat worked as he swallowed. "You'd have to actually give this a shot, though," he said, leaning closer. His breath puffed lightly across her lips.

Her mouth opened, but then she stepped back, letting her hands fall to her sides. "What would that even mean?" She shook her head, crossing the couple steps to the dark end of the porch. "I work, and when I'm not at work, I'm with Parker. And school's out soon, which means even at work, I'll have Parker." Every summer, she'd settle him at one of the smaller tables with a bunch of activity books from the dollar store. Spelling, and reading, and even math if she could find them. At least one person in their family would make it to college.

"Yeah, and I have a life, too," Bobby said behind her. "A job, even. Hell,"—his hand landed on her shoulder, prompting her to turn around—"we're heading out on tour in something like ten days."

"Right." Dennings had mentioned it, the tour they did out on the West Coast every summer. And touring meant girls throwing themselves at the band. Pretty, uncomplicated ones. "So maybe we just wait," Liz Anne said. Made even less sense to start something before he left, anyway. "See where things stand when you're back."

It'd give him time to think better of it all, too. Bobby might be too nice to back off right after hearing her story, but a month from now? He'd think better of it, find some way to let her down easy.

Liz Anne moved back to the bench and sank down, too heavy with exhaustion to keep standing. Best she could hope for when reality came crashing down around all these maybes was that he'd let her pay for a lesson here and there, if she could scrounge up the money. It'd even be easier, probably, if he was seeing someone else by that point.

She shut her eyes at the soft thuds of Bobby's steps. But he stopped at her side and sat down. "Sounds like a cop out," he said.

A couple seconds passed as Liz Anne let her head droop lower. Then she pulled her shoulders back and looked straight at Bobby. "It's a way out."

Bobby's jaw clenched at the dismissal. But then he shook his head and leaned back on the bench, looking out at nothing in particular. "From giving this a shot to running scared in under five minutes…"

He could practically feel her frowning at him. "I'm not scared," she said.

He hummed like he believed her.

"Our lives, they don't mix," she insisted, her voice a little thicker.

Bobby dropped the casual act with a sigh. He turned toward her, tucking one leg under him. When he took her hand, she bristled beside him. But she didn't let go, so he wove her cold fingers in between his warmer ones, leaning his free arm on the back of the bench. "They could."

Her gaze jumped from him, down to their linked hands. "How?" she breathed.

He wrapped his free arm around her shoulders and tugged her closer. She hesitated, posture growing even stiffer, until an exhale sagged her against him. Bobby smiled, giving her fingers a light squeeze. "Not like you live on the other side of the country." Like Kane and Sabella had, when they'd met. "Hell, there ain't even a whole state between us. And I don't mind driving out here, if that's your next big hurdle."

She chuckled quietly, but didn't try to argue. So maybe he was making some headway.

"I don't even mind hanging out with Parker, once you're okay with that. Or as your friend-slash-guitar-teacher. Might even be good for him," Bobby teased, "having someone less uptight around."

Liz Anne's mouth popped open, and she made a move to elbow him, but Bobby hugged her closer so she couldn't. She settled for claiming, "I am not uptight."

"Yeah, you are. But it's okay, we'll work on it." He winked to rile her up. But she only smiled, rolling her eyes with a small headshake.

With her tension worked out a bit, Bobby shifted them on the bench so she was half lying on it, curled against his chest. "Maybe someday," he continued, "you could find a job out in Nashville, move closer. Get a publishing deal, maybe, for your songs, work on your music… That's what you want, right? To get out of here with your son. Or all three of you."

She nodded, her hair tickling his neck.

"And since I'd be around, I could help. Keep an eye out for jobs, introduce you to folks." To music people, sure, but the parents he knew were always helping each other out with their kids, which would make things easier for her, too. And if down the line they moved in together… Well, then he'd be there for the both of them.

But he was getting ahead of himself. "Meanwhile," he said, getting back on track, "we'd just see how things go."

Liz Anne shifted so she could look up at him. Half her face was hidden in shadows, but the longing was still clear.

"Doesn't sound too bad, right?" he said.

"Sounds…amazing," she whispered back.

She wasn't wrong.

Bobby swallowed, pushing aside the picture he'd painted of the future to focus on the fact they were together, right now. He bent down, brushing his lips against hers a few times. She arched closer, and he deepened the kiss, sinking into the silken feel, the almost peachy taste of her.

By the time the kiss ended, his breath was coming faster, and the illuminated side of her face was flushed. He straightened, dropping a light kiss against her temple. "If all that," he said, then paused to swallow past the hoarseness. "If that's a future you want, well…"

"Well?" She stared up at him, eyes wide, more vulnerable than he'd seen her anywhere except on stage.

He smiled, brushing a loose strand of hair back from her forehead. "Then you gotta be willing to take a chance."

<h1 style="text-align:center">Epilogue</h1>

He's here!" Parker jumped down from his lookout spot on the couch and finally let the curtain drift shut.

He was almost out the door when Liz Anne called, "Wait." Ignoring the ripple of anticipation in her gut, she finished placing the caramel chocolate chip cookies in the waiting ziplock bag.

Parker turned and fixed her with his little impatient stare. "Will you tell me now?"

"And here I thought you liked surprises," she teased. And she had a great one in store for him today. Parker knew Bobby would be hanging out with them, but he had no idea they were off to Franklin on the 4th, with its pony rides and petting zoo and tons of other fun promised. It was going to be way better than their usual celebration—hanging out in their own back-yard. They usually couldn't afford much, so soon after Parker's birthday. But she'd set aside what she could of her tips so they could splurge a little today. Even she was excited, but that might have been about finally seeing Bobby again.

Sure, they'd talked and texted while he was out on tour, but it wasn't the same. The little time they'd spent together before he left had been tinged with the reminder that they didn't have long. But now, he was back. And he'd decided to spend the holiday with her and Parker. Seemed like a good sign. Of course, maybe he was back to just being nice.

"Go grab us some water bottles, please," she said, turning Parker toward the pantry. He ran off as Bobby knocked. Liz Anne swung the door open, letting her stuffed backpack drop to the floor.

"Hey." His smile was exactly as she remembered, cheeky and easygoing. Just like the rest of him, casually relaxed in his usual jeans and a tee shirt.

"Hi," she answered with a small smile of her own.

His eyes dipped to her mouth, then lower, taking in her tank top and denim skirt. The tension between them grew warmer, sending a fresh swell of anticipation through her. Bobby seemed about to kiss her when Parker appeared at her side.

Liz Anne took a half step back from the doorway. "Parker, you remember Mister Bobby, right?" she asked, helping him put the water bottles in with the rest of their supplies, from cookies to sunscreen.

"Hello," he said, much more solemnly than minutes ago.

"Hey." Bobby crouched down. "You excited to hang out today?"

Parker's shoulder inched up. His eyes darted between her and Bobby.

"We sure are," Liz Anne said.

Bobby's eyebrows shot up with his frown. She shrugged back. What could she say? Apparently being excited for an Independence Day surprise was different than being excited to see Bobby, even if Parker had known both those things were happening together. Seemed it had been long enough since Memorial Day that he was back to feeling shy. Was she doing this wrong, having him and Bobby spend time together so soon?

"What do you got there?" Bobby asked, taking a different tack.

Parker was still hanging on to the strap of her bag, and he pulled it closer. "Water and stuff." He brightened as he remembered, "Momma made cookies."

"Oh yeah? Think you'll be up for sharing?"

"Yeah," Parker declared and started trying to open the backpack again to get the cookies out. Bobby straightened from his crouch, smiling down at her son.

"O-okay." Liz Anne set a hand on Parker's arm. "Maybe we should actually make it out of the house before digging in to the cookies. You ready to go?" she added as his posture sagged.

"Now?" he asked. The pain of waiting crossing his face almost made her relent.

"How about in the car," she offered. He immediately ran out to wait by Bobby's truck.

"He still doesn't know?" Bobby asked while Liz Anne locked the door.

"It's like I'm torturing him." Bobby reached for the back-pack, and she added, "You don't need to do that."

"I'll trade you." He pulled something out of his pocket and held his clenched fist in front of her. A moment later, a charm fell from his fingers, dangling on a leather strap.

Liz Anne stilled the swinging charm between her fingers, revealing a dark-blue guitar pick, with a little silver music note attached. "Wow," she breathed. When was the last time some-one other than her family had given her a gift?

"Oh, and…" Bobby let the necklace go and used his freed fingers to tilt her chin up. "Hi," he repeated before stepping close to kiss her.

Since Parker was blocked from seeing by Bobby's shoul-ders, she let the kiss linger for a couple seconds.

When it ended, Bobby said, "Now we can go." He jogged down the porch steps without waiting for a reply. Liz Anne slipped the necklace over her ponytail and followed.

"Do *you* know where we're going?" Parker asked once they'd all gotten in the car.

"Well I better, since I'm driving," Bobby said. The engine purred to life. "You ready to tell him?"

Liz Anne twisted to catch Parker's expression. "We are going over to Franklin, for a big, city-wide Fourth of July party, with music, and food, and even a special kids-only parade. And so much other cool stuff." Bobby'd mentioned some of the fam-ilies from the barbecue might even come out, so Parker might have some familiar faces to play with for once.

A grin split his little face. "Really?"

She grinned back, patting his knee. "Really."

"How far's Franklin?" Parker asked, already staring out the window.

"Don't you worry," Bobby said with his own smile. "We have the whole entire day to do everything fun we can think of."

"Cool," Parker whispered, slumping back into the seat even while his legs vibrated with excitement.

Liz Anne resettled in her seat too, facing forward as the truck sped up.

"What about you," Bobby asked quietly beside her, tossing a glance her way. "You excited?"

Liz Anne fingered the guitar-pick charm around her neck. "Can't wait."

From My Lips
    by Liz Anne Layton

When the sun sinks down low,
And the world goes dark
When I'm broken apart,
And I've lost my spark
Desperate, I try to believe
Somehow you could hear me
Quiet pleas fall from my lips,
Fly from my lips to heaven

When I picture your face,
How your eyes shine bright
My arms ache to hold you
Keep you safe through the night
Desperate, I try to believe
You'll soon be here with me
My prayers pour out from my lips,
Fly from my lips to heaven

My heart can't beat, while we're apart
I miss your love, as I seek a fresh start
For us

Desperate, I try to believe
Somehow you could hear me
And whispered pleas fall from my lips

— Acknowledgements —

Heartfelt thanks to—

Kris: this story wouldn't be the same without your help.

Rachel: for never losing enthusiasm for my writing.

Gwen L.P.: for her extensive knowledge of hymns and help finding the perfect one.

My writing group: for willingly diving into the incredibly rough first draft.

Christa at Paper & Sage: for another perfect cover—you read my mind!

And especially those who stood by me through my recent hardships. You know who you are.

Read on for an excerpt from
Forging Forever, book 1:

Mending Heartstrings

One

Kane walked out of the private back room of Nashville's Fiddle and Steel and headed straight for the bar. Every so often, he'd still try out his new material at their open mic nights. But tonight, the initially warm reception of the regulars had fizzled out as he played. They hadn't really responded to any of his three songs. He needed a beer.

A couple of the regulars greeted him, and Kane paused to exchange pleasantries. The laid-back atmosphere of the bar put everyone at ease, which was the great thing about playing there. The locals who knew him weren't intimidated by his relative fame, and he wasn't a big enough deal yet for the occasional tourist to recognize him. He relied on the reactions of this comfortable community. And they sure didn't mind telling him he had more work to do before his next tour.

When he finally reached the bar, he flagged down Cody, tearing the younger man away from a pretty brunette who was probably underage. He greeted Kane with a subtle lift of his chin.

"How's it going, man?" Kane asked.

"Just got better," Cody answered, looking over Kane's shoulder.

Kane followed his gaze to a group of women who'd just walked in but turned back after barely a moment. He definitely wouldn't mind a distraction. First, though, he really did want that beer. "Get your mind back on your work, boy," Kane scolded with a smile.

Cody's mama hadn't raised an idiot. "You just want them for yourself."

Kane grinned. "It's no competition."

"Only 'cause those three didn't hear you flame out tonight."

"Yeah, well. Some of us can rely on our good looks." Kane kept an easy smile on his face. The ribbing shouldn't have bothered him, but he was having an off night. The songs he'd played could have passed muster most anywhere else, but Nashville knew its country music. "Get me a beer, would ya?" he asked.

"Yeah, yeah." Cody slapped a coaster onto the bar in front of Kane then headed to the fridge to grab Kane's favorite.

Kane rested his forearms on the bar and bent his head down, exhaling. As always, he'd scanned the audience a few times while he played, trying to read the room's reactions. Tonight, too many people had been absorbed in their own conversations around the bar's simple wooden tables. Only one pair of eyes had met his. A striking, unwavering pair of eyes.

She'd been standing toward the back, alone. He'd felt her watching him even when he'd closed his eyes.

But she hadn't been standing there when he'd come back out. Probably just as well.

Cody set down a chilled beer in front of Kane. He tipped it toward the bartender as thanks. A couple drinks, a little bit of flirting, and there'd be no more need to think about his songs tonight.

Turning back toward the room, Kane bumped a girl he hadn't noticed seated next to him at the bar. "Ah! Sorry 'bout that," he said with a half-smile, ramping up the charm.

She twisted toward him. "I'll survive." The corners of her mouth pulled up, but Kane couldn't look away from her eyes. *Hazel*, he realized. Unlike when he'd been on stage, her gaze fell, and she started to turn back to the bar.

"Kane," he offered, shifting his beer to his left hand and offering up his right. *A handshake. Smooth.* This really was an off night.

Her eyes flicked down to his hand then laughingly back to his face. Her eyebrows drew up in a small challenge as she placed her hand in his. "Like the sugar, or the stick?"

"With a K…" He leaned back against the bar, resting on one elbow.

"So, not Abel's brother. Good to know."

Normally he'd have walked away at a line like that, but it wasn't like he'd been offering conversational gold. Maybe this would help him shake it off before he made his move on the trio Cody'd pointed out. And then there were those eyes… "Go ahead and joke. I've probably heard them all."

"Don't tempt me." Her lips curved softly. Mischief glinted in her eyes.

"And how could I do that?" Kane let himself relax, sliding back into the easy feel of the bar. Unlike his performance, this conversation didn't really matter.

"I'm sure you have a few tricks up your sleeves." She picked up the glass of white wine she'd been nursing and took a sip, without dropping her smile or taking her eyes off him.

A local girl would've been drinking beer. But then, a local girl would've known exactly who he was, which could lead to nothing more than a mildly satisfying romp in the sack. He remembered his own beer and took a swig.

"Worried?" he asked, after she set her glass back down.

That got him a bigger smile. "Please, I can take anything you throw at me."

"Maybe we should test that theory." He took another sip of beer. This was getting more and more interesting.

"By all means," she replied, not missing a beat.

He was used to women flattering him, fawning over him. His Southern charm had rarely failed him, and as a singer, he wasn't hurting for female attention, especially since country music wannabes thought he'd be a perfect springboard for their careers. But he hadn't met someone who actually intrigued him in a while. Too long.

He turned to face her, leaving his elbow resting on the bar, and set down his beer. "I didn't catch your name."

"Call me Elle," she answered, tilting her head slightly, a silent question on the change in direction. Her eyelashes didn't flutter with calculated coyness, and her direct gaze didn't falter.

Kane straightened, suddenly inspired. "Pleased to meet you, Elle. Excuse me a sec?" He grabbed the bottle he'd just set down and turned away from her. Another swig and he returned to the back room. This was nothing short of crazy, but he picked up his guitar anyway and walked back to the small stage.

Sabella had barely returned to her wine when she heard the slight strumming of a guitar as someone settled in front of the microphone. She wasn't certain what had prompted Kane to leave so abruptly, but she was definitely disappointed. Not that she was star-struck or anything. The fact that she had dressed up to venture outside her hotel room, to the Fiddle and Steel Guitar Bar, simply because she had heard that Kane Hartridge would possibly be trying out new material at their open mic night, did *not* mean she was star-struck. If anything, she was underwhelmed by his song choices tonight, and even more so by her awkward attempt at flirting. Men like Kane didn't waste their attentions on women like her.

She took another sip of the perfectly nice Riesling and silently deliberated whether she would stay past draining her glass. This bar did have a certain, inexplicably innate, country charm that she wouldn't mind exploring and observing further. After all, she had come to Nashville to learn what she could about the culture of country music.

As far as she could tell, the room around her was furnished with exactly the same style of unadorned, wooden furniture and boasted a similar smattering of booths around the perimeter as any other bar. Nothing about the décor particularly screamed "country." No posters of country stars lined the walls, and if it weren't for the distinct twang emanating from the patrons' conversations and through the speakers, she could have been back home. If she could figure out what exactly made this bar so popular among the locals, the night wouldn't have to be a complete waste. Plus, her flight the next day wasn't until the afternoon, so she could afford to stay out awhile.

"Hey, guys." Kane's voice carried through the speaker system, quieting the room. Someone shut off the recorded music that had been playing ever since he had left the small stage, his performance intended as the finale of their open mic night. Sabella twisted on her barstool to face the stage. Kane and his guitar once again occupied the unadorned chair set behind the single microphone. His beer bottle rested just behind his leg. "Don't mean to pull y'all away, but I have a friend in from out of town who is dyin', she's absolutely dyin', to sing for you. Please join me in welcomin' Elle—over by the bar, there, in the purple, that's Elle—welcomin' her to the Fiddle an' Steel stage."

Most of the patrons shifted their attention toward the bar, trying to find Kane's "friend." Sabella froze, schooling her expression. *I can take anything you throw at me*, she had said. He was clearly testing her claim. What in the world had she been thinking?

"C'mon, Elle," Kane called through the microphone. "Here's your chance." His mouth pulled into a half smile, intended to portray solicitous charm, no doubt, not the baiting nature of his challenge.

She took a deep breath, reminding herself she would likely never see any of these people again, and slid off the barstool. Apparently, her customarily rigid practicality had been dislodged the second he'd bumped into her. Not that he was giving her much choice.

The stage was closer than she would have preferred, but the walk over from the bar still gave Sabella plenty of time to admire Kane's comfortable posture. He wore jeans and a faded, black, button-down shirt, with a few buttons left unfastened and rolled-up sleeves. With his brown hair cut raggedly to slightly above his ears in front, somewhat longer in back, and his stunning green eyes, he really was more handsome than any man had a right to be. Especially one who was trying to embarrass her in front of a bar full of people.

"What exactly do you have in mind?" she murmured as she took the short step onto the stage.

He covered the microphone. "Name a country duet."

At least he wasn't going to force her to sing alone. Still, she wasn't exactly a country music savant. "The only one that comes to mind is 'Picture.'" That wasn't strictly speaking true, but she was betting he would be even less thrilled with her choice if she had named one with Kelly Clarkson.

All Kane said was, "All right." He shifted his chair so it wasn't squarely facing the microphone then started to play an intro. "Not the newest song in the book, but a guilty pleasure for some of y'all, I'm sure," he drawled, smiling at the crowd.

His voice captured her as he sang, its purity reminding her why his was the only country music to which she really listened. As she watched him, Sabella almost forgot he had manipulated her into joining him on stage—for a *duet*. She looked out over their somewhat captive audience, filled with men in worn-out jeans and flannel shirts—even a cowboy hat or two—and some amazingly beautiful women. Maybe this was actually a bizarre dream, and in reality she was sleeping in her hotel room, or even back home in her bed. If only.

When Kane finished the first chorus, he looked up at her in anticipation. Little crinkles appeared around his eyes. He didn't think she would do it.

To be fair, normally she wouldn't have. *This is simply a more active form of research,* she assured herself. Sticky sweat still gathered between her fingers and coated her palms. Sabella surreptitiously wiped her hands on her thighs and stepped marginally closer to the microphone.

She scrambled to remember the lyrics, staring at the floor as she sang. When no one booed by the end of the stanza, she risked a glance out at the room. About half of the tables had reverted to quiet conversation, but others appeared to be listening. At the end of her chorus, she looked over at Kane.

He was watching her, eyebrows drawn slightly together, as if he wasn't altogether sure what he was seeing. Maybe he was shocked she was still singing, despite the blatant difference in their abilities. She had never been one for public displays of foolery, and the remaining shreds of her rationality were appalled by the ridiculousness of her behavior. Running off the stage would be worse, though, or at the very least more memorable.

She finished their interchanging lines with her eyes on him. The last chord he strummed hung in the air until the murmuring of patrons' conversations wiped it away. Sabella backed away from Kane and the microphone, then turned to step off the stage, and wove her way toward the hallway that led to the bar's restrooms and a door with an "Employees Only" sign. She pressed her back to the wall for support and resolutely steadied her breathing. This night wasn't turning out anything like she could have expected.

✧ ✧ ✧

Kane stayed on stage through the applause that started just as Elle left. It was more applause than he'd gotten alone tonight, not that he was surprised. She sang purely, without flourish. She sure wouldn't be making a career of this, but something about her singing had captivated their audience, and him. It was so…earnest. Unassuming. Maybe that's what he had glimpsed in her eyes.

Falling back on his ingrained charm, Kane offered a smile and a "good night" to the audience. He followed Elle's route to the bar's back rooms, taking his guitar with him. Cody might whine later that he'd left the beer for the boy to pick up, but Kane didn't care.

He found her leaning against the wall that faced the ladies' room. "Waiting for a friend?"

Her head jerked toward him. She straightened from the wall and turned to face him. "Did you enjoy the show?" She wasn't smiling now.

A Southern girl would've chewed his hide for that stunt. And if she really hadn't wanted to sing, she would've found a way to bow out, or plain old told him to go to hell.

"You surprised me," he answered honestly. "You have a nice voice." *And gumption.*

"That's somewhat patronizing coming from you, don't you think?"

He smiled. "A fan, are you?" he teased, though she obviously wasn't. But that suited him just fine.

She raised her eyebrows. A second later her shoulders shrugged, and she looked down. He was pretty sure he saw a hint of a smile.

"C'mon," he said then turned toward the private room to put away his guitar. Maybe this night had potential yet.

———~———

Mending Heartstrings (Forging Forever, book 1)
is available everywhere books are sold.

— About Aria —

Aria Glazki's first kiss technically came from a bear cub. Though no fairytale transformation followed, she still believes magic can happen when the right people come together—if they don't get in their own way, that is. So now Aria writes heartfelt romances about relatable people overcoming real-world obstacles to build love that lasts.

Learn more about Aria and her books at:
www.AriaGlazki.com

www.ingramcontent.com/pod-product-compliance
Lightning Source LLC
Chambersburg PA
CBHW050408190726
48284CB00007BB/2484